*A
Harlequin
Romance*

THE
BLACK DELANEY

by

HENRIETTA REID

HARLEQUIN BOOKS
WINNIPEG ● **CANADA**

First published in 1970 by Mills & Boon Limited,
17 - 19 Foley Street, London, England.

SBN 373-01460-0

© Henrietta Reid 1970

Harlequin Canadian edition published January, 1971
Harlequin U.S. edition published April, 1971

Printed in Canada

1460

CHAPTER ONE

'So you see, Nicola,' Aunt Doris said decisively, 'after Joyce's marriage I shan't need you any more.' One hand fidgeted with the gold bracelet that encircled her plump wrist. 'You must realize,' she went on hurriedly, as I gazed at her in stricken silence, 'that it's simply not practical for me to remain on here when Joyce marries and has a home of her own. Not that I intend to live with her and Geoffrey, of course. I hope I've too much sense to do that! But I thought of going to a small private hotel on the east coast. Some place not too expensive where I'd get personal attention and my little whims catered for.'

She laughed lightly, but I knew from experience that Aunt Doris expected her whims to be taken very seriously indeed.

'But what am I to do?' I asked desperately. 'I thought you'd stay on here at The Hollies: that it held memories of Uncle Victor. At least you always said so,' I added lamely.

She turned her pale eyes on me with an expression of cold affront. 'Really, Nicola,' she said frigidly, 'surely you don't expect me to spend my remaining days in mourning for your uncle? Anyway, he'd have been the last to expect it.' She glanced fleetingly in the mirror above the mantelpiece. 'After all, although I may appear ancient to a young girl like you, I am not exactly decrepit.'

'It's just that I don't know what I'll do,' I protested.

'I've been so busy helping Joyce with her trousseau.'

Aunt Doris nodded and reached for a cigarette. 'Naturally! After all, it was understood when I adopted you that when the time came you'd pull your weight. 'And I don't deny,' she added graciously, 'that you've been a great help, especially where Joyce has been concerned. She's so pretty and wilful, and used to getting her own way.' She smiled fondly. 'But then so was I at her age.'

But not half so pretty, I thought, regarding my aunt's round moon-like face with the small podgy nose and tight stubborn mouth.

Outside dusk was beginning to settle on the lawn and the first hint of autumn made the high-ceilinged room chill and bleak. In the fireplace kindling had been stacked, but Aunt Doris didn't believe in lighting fires until winter was properly established.

For the first time in all my years at The Hollies I fully realized how little I counted for in the household.

'You mustn't think I haven't provided for your future,' my aunt continued defensively. 'I should hope I know my duty to poor dear Victor's niece better than that. As soon as I made up my mind to let The Hollies I got in touch with the Delaneys in Ireland. After all, they're relations of yours and owe you a certain amount of consideration.'

I gazed at her in astonishment. 'But Uncle Victor told me that he and my mother were the last of the Rochfords.'

She shook her head impatiently. 'When I say relations, I mean that the connection is very slight indeed, and only through another branch of the family. I'm

6

afraid your uncle preferred not to mention them. There was some sort of scandal. I believe they're a wild lawless breed, not at all the kind Victor cared to associate with. But I'm afraid there wasn't anyone else I could think of. After all, you're very young and you haven't really trained for any particular career, have you?'

Except to be a lady's maid to Cousin Joyce, I thought bitterly.

Aunt Doris polished her lacquered fingernails on the arm, of her chair. 'And anyway, beggars——' She stopped and had the grace to flush slightly.

'Beggars can't be choosers,' I concluded stonily.

She shrugged. 'We must be realistic about these matters, my dear. I'm perfectly certain you and I could have settled down together after Joyce's marriage, but as I told you, it's absolutely impossible to stay on here, and I'm sure you'll be a sensible girl and try to make the best of things. After all, you needn't stay on with the Delaneys unless you want to, but until you have obtained more experience of the world it might be as well for you to try and adapt yourself.'

She crossed the room to the small elegant French desk at which she did her correspondence and, reaching in, extracted an envelope. She unfolded a letter and perused it for a moment frowningly. 'This is the reply I received to the letter I sent to Rowan Delaney, who appears to be the present head of the family. His address is Raheen Castle. Pity his manners are not in keeping with his background! He appears to be a complete boor. However, he says he will be in England in about a fortnight's time and will collect you on the way back.'

'Collect me!' I repeated.

She glanced up with a look of abstracted irritation. 'Please don't be obstructive, Nicola. You must realize I had some difficulty in locating the man in the first place. I may say also that I don't relish being treated in a cavalier fashion by this boorish Irishman.' As she spoke she glanced at the letter again and flushed, and it was clear that her eye had fallen on some particularly offensive sentence. As she had not offered to let me read the letter it was only too plain that the remarks in it were anything but complimentary concerning my proposed stay with the Delaneys at Raheen Castle.

So I was to be collected, like an unwanted parcel, by Rowan Delaney! I felt an angry antagonism sweep over me in great waves. I would show this Rowan Delaney that I had as little desire to be his guest as he had to receive me!

Aunt Doris folded the letter and replaced it in her desk. 'The arrogance of the man! If he didn't want to take you he could have said so without being gratuitously insulting!'

'He can hardly be keen on the idea of having an unknown and unwanted relation foisted upon him,' I said drily.

'According to your uncle the Delaneys are a clannish breed,' Aunt Doris said sharply, 'and if that is the case they ought to accept the kinship. After all, you have a certain amount of Delaney blood in your veins.'

'A little more and I might have inherited something of the Delaney independence,' I said.

She frowned. 'This is something I meant to speak to you about, Nicola. I don't know if you are aware of it, but you're extremely sharp-tongued at times. In fact you've often wounded poor Joyce, without altogether realizing it, I'm sure. But then she's an extraordinarily sensitive girl—like myself in that way. A cruel look or word can cut me to the quick. Your sharp manner is naturally not going to endear you to the Delaneys, so if I were you I'd put a curb on my tongue, and try to be as pleasant and adaptable as possible. The Delaneys appear to be well off and have a position of influence in the west of Ireland. Who knows,' she added vaguely, 'perhaps in time you might meet someone suitable and settle down. The whole thing is probably for the best. If you find this Rowan Delaney too unpleasant, you can always contrive to keep out of his way. After all, in a castle there should be ample space.'

I felt a growing curiosity concerning Rowan Delaney. Was he young, old, ugly or handsome? For some reason I suddenly felt it was important that I should know. The knowledge would give me a key as to how I should behave when he collected me—as he had expressed it.

My aunt shook her head when I asked her. 'As to his age, I haven't the remotest idea, but your uncle said they were a remarkably handsome family, very dark—almost foreignly so. They have a bad history, I believe. Your uncle wasn't specific.' She looked down primly. 'But I gathered the Delaneys are womanizers and have a reputation for lawlessness. Of course,' she added hastily as she saw my expression, 'he was speaking about the last generation. For all I know Rowan Delaney may be a paragon of all the virtues.'

'Considering the tone of his letter, it hardly seems likely,' I said wryly.

Again a frown creased her forehead at what she took to be my lack of co-operation and I could see she was relieved when a diversion was caused by a loud knocking from the floor above. She said hurriedly, 'The wreath for Joyce's wedding veil has arrived and I'm sure she wants you to see it. You'd better go up now. You know how she hates being kept waiting.'

As I made my way upstairs I was thinking that not only did Joyce hate being kept waiting but she hated repairing her clothes or keeping her room in any sort of order and in fact hated doing any boring tedious chores while I was there to do them. Then with a feeling of surprise it struck me that I wouldn't be there to do them much longer. Very shortly I would be borne off by the unknown Rowan Delaney to his castle in the west of Ireland. I had never been to Ireland and couldn't even imagine what life would be like there, but Aunt Doris had made it plain that Raheen Castle was in a wild and remote part. For the first time I felt apprehensive. It might be true that, as my aunt said, I had a sharp tongue, but what defence would it be against this Rowan Delaney if he lived up to the family reputation?

When I opened the door of Joyce's room I found her seated at the dressing-table. Her bedroom was the largest in the house. Even my aunt's was much inferior in size and furnishings to her daughter's.

Joyce turned round impatiently as I came in. 'Oh, there you are. Did you not hear me knock?'

'I did,' I said coolly. 'I came as fast as I could. Did you think I was going to fly upstairs?'

She raised her eyebrows. 'Dear me, we do sound uppity! What's come over you?'

'Nothing really,' I said bleakly, 'except that I won't have to put up with your moods and tenses much longer.'

She smiled tightly as she turned her head from side to side before the mirror, studying the effect of a wreath of mock orange blossom against her hair. 'What do you think of it?' she asked dubiously.

In the triple mirrors of her dressing-table her small pretty face was reflected. In spite of her querulous manner she looked round-faced and girlish. 'It's very pretty,' I said.

'Um,' she demurred. 'Personally I think the blossoms look too small.'

'No, they're just right,' I said. 'You don't want the wreath to take attention away from the veil.'

'No, that's true,' she agreed. 'It belonged to Geoffrey's mother and is really something of an heirloom.'

Reluctantly she removed the wreath from her head and wrapped it carefully in tissue paper. 'You'll be staying for the wedding, won't you?'

So Joyce had been aware of the plans that had been going forward about my future, although Aunt Doris hadn't bothered to tell me, I thought bitterly. I shook my head. 'No, I'll be gone before then.'

'Oh, but I wanted you to be here for the wedding,' she protested. 'You could have helped me to dress. I know you would have seen everything was just perfect: you're that sort of person.'

'Am I?' I said dryly. 'Then perhaps it's just as well I'm making a change. I don't want to end up as a well-trained lady's maid.'

For the first time she regarded me with real interest.

'Mother told me she was getting in touch with the Delaneys, but I didn't realize everything would happen so soon. They sound a horrid family and I'm sorry—really sorry, Nicola—that you're going to them. I mean, you've always been frightfully decent to me, and I know I've been a bit of a pig at times.'

I gazed at her in amazement. Not for a moment had I considered Joyce capable of expressing remorse.

'Don't look so surprised,' she said swiftly. 'I'm very much in love with Geoffrey, you know. I want to start afresh: I don't want to turn into a shrew of a wife and make him miserable. You see, I suddenly realized the other day that I'm growing very much like Mother. She led Daddy a dog's life and I know he was wretchedly unhappy, although Mother didn't seem to realize it.'

It was true, I thought. Uncle Victor had not lived long after I had joined the household at The Hollies, but I could remember the sad, resigned lines on his kindly face whenever his wife came on the scene with her bustling, domineering manner and her strident voice.

'I'm sorry too I won't be here for your wedding,' I said a little gruffly, trying to hide how ridiculously elated I was at this display of friendship—although Joyce's sudden show of remorse might be due to the fact that in future the Irish Sea would flow between us, I told myself a little cynically.

'How do you feel about going to these Delaney people?' she asked curiously. 'I never quite know how you feel about things: you're inclined to be secretive. Although, looking back, I realize one can hardly blame you.'

CHAPTER TWO

For the next fortnight Aunt Doris saw to it that I was kept too busily employed to let my thoughts linger on the arrival of Rowan Delaney. In preparation for her departure and the letting of The Hollies she began a thorough cleaning of cupboards and drawers, and gradually it began to dawn on me what an acquisitive woman Aunt Doris really was. She had hoarded the most useless objects in the fond hope that some day she might have need of them. I could see it was quite a wrench for her to consign to the flames the odds and ends that she had lived with for years. Frequently she asked my advice concerning some article and was quite affronted when I advised consigning it to the rubbish heap.

'Really, Nicola,' she said pettishly when she had tossed a pair of ancient kid gloves into the large basket which was rapidly filling with junk of every description, 'I've come to the conclusion that you've no heart. No sensitiveness! That's what makes it so difficult for you to understand my feelings. These gloves, shabby as they may be, were those I wore the first time I met your Uncle Victor. Right away, he remarked how tiny my hands are.' She glanced down at them complacently.

'But you said yourself you were putting the past behind you and starting afresh,' I reminded her wearily.

She sniffed. 'Maybe so, but it's easier said than done.' Then her face puckered ominously and she dabbed at her eyes with a tiny lace-edged handkerchief.

I gazed at her impatiently. All day long we had gone from room to room on the dreary business of winding up a lifetime, and as the house became gradually bare and austere I felt more and more the cold winter of change. Where would I be when new inhabitants took over and impressed their characters on these rooms?

I began to dread the arrival of Rowan Delaney and felt a growing panic as the days seemed to rush past in a flurry of activity. Joyce was too taken up with her approaching marriage to give more than passing attention to our activities, although she did mention to Geoffrey the plans her mother had made for my future.

He gazed at me solemnly through his glasses. 'Um, I can't say I think it's particularly wise of your mother if this Delaney crowd are as wild and unconventional as you say,' he told Joyce. His pale eyes scanned me briefly. 'I can see no reason why Nicola can't come into the office. We need extra staff and she'd probably be very useful.'

'There's always the small point that I know neither shorthand nor typing,' I said bluntly, resentful of being discussed as if I were one of Aunt Doris's unfortunate acquisitions to be disposed of as quickly and discreetly as possible.

Perversely I dug my heels in stubbornly when he added magnanimously, 'I'd be perfectly willing to arrange a secretarial course for Nicola. She could gradually repay me when she goes on salary. It's a much more sensible idea than your mother's. After all, you're a young and pretty girl, Nicola.' Again he shot a quick glance in my direction and coughed judiciously.

'You might find yourself in an extraordinarily un-pleasant and compromising situation with these De-laneys.'

Much as I dreaded the advent of Rowan Delaney and my unknown future, I hated the idea of being incarcerated in Geoffrey's musty office and continually subject to his condescension and criticism.

'It wouldn't work out,' I said quickly. 'I know I'd make a simply rotten secretary. Besides,' I added wildly, 'I can't spell and my punctuation is dreadful.'

He smiled and smoothed back his hair complacently. 'I'm perfectly willing to be patient with you—at the beginning at least,' he added hastily. 'Afterwards, as you improved, you could take on more responsibility. I think I can safely say that you'll find the work extra-ordinarily interesting.'

'Nicola's right,' Joyce put in a little sharply. 'Frankly, I don't imagine she'd have any talent for the legal business. Apart from that, all the plans are made for Rowan Delaney to pick her up here and take her with him to Ireland.'

He glanced at his watch. 'I'd better be off! Well, I've done my best. Not many men in my position would have even considered taking on someone com-pletely untrained. However, if you're adamant——' He paused.

'I am,' I said firmly. 'Everyone at The Hollies will be beginning a new way of life. I don't want to tag along like a sort of left-over whom no one knows.'

'Oh, if that's how you feel——!' he shrugged.

'Nicola's grateful, of course,' Joyce put in soothingly, 'but I must say I agree with her. It's much better to make a completely new break. And now, Geoffrey darling, isn't it time you and I discussed our plans?' She tucked her arm through his and glanced at me significantly. And, taking the hint, I left them together.

As the end of the second week approached and there was no sign of Rowan Delaney I began to feel a certain relief. He had made no secret in his letter to Aunt Doris of his reluctance to take me into his home. Obviously he had now decided to renege.

Aunt Doris kept glancing through the windows overlooking the short drive; then, as it dawned on her that Rowan Delaney had backed out of the arrangement, she grew peevish and silent as she realized I was not to be as easily disposed of as she had thought.

Strangely enough I felt a sense of anti-climax. What sort of man was he who had so boldly slashed his handwriting across the envelope my aunt had taken from her desk? One thing was certain, he was arrogant and ill-mannered; the type of man I would always have to be on the defensive with. It was as well he had changed his mind, as I would have disliked him intensely.

Then, without warning, he arrived.

I was in Joyce's room helping her with a list of wedding invitations. Earlier that day I had spent several hours in the attic with Aunt Doris listing furniture that she intended sending in for auction, and I felt tired and untidy from hours of rummaging and listening to Aunt Doris wavering indecisively over each object before making up her mind. It had been a relief when Joyce had asked me to help her with the list.

From my seat near the window I chanced to look out and saw without interest that a large powerful-looking car was moving along the drive. As Aunt Doris led a pretty active social life I merely assumed the car contained some of her friends and went back to my list without giving it more than a passing glance.

It was only when the daily woman tapped at the door and announced that Mr Delaney had arrived and that I was wanted downstairs that I realized with sick dismay that Rowan Delaney had at last decided to collect me.

I gave a quick glance in the mirror before following her, and fumbled with the elastic band that I had used to pull back my hair. There was a streak of dust across my left cheek and I rubbed at it frantically with a tissue I found on the dressing-table.

'For heaven's sake,' Joyce laughed without humour, 'do you really think this Delaney man is going to care how you look? He probably intends you to pull your weight when you get to Raheen Castle and won't expect you to look like a beauty queen.'

'Maybe so,' I said, 'but I'm not facing him looking like Cinderella.'

Joyce shrugged indifferently and returned to her list, and I slowly walked downstairs.

I could feel my heart beating nervously as I approached the drawing-room door. It stood ajar and I could hear my aunt talking excitedly and a man's deep abrupt voice answering her. Then, straightening myself, I pushed open the door and went in. For a moment I stood, feeling a sense of shock as I saw the tall, dark-haired, broad-shouldered man who stood with his back to the fireplace. Even in the big high-ceilinged drawing-room he seemed to dwarf everything about him. Aunt Doris barely came up to his shoulder and the dark, strong-featured face was regarding her with

19

an expression that was grim and saturnine.

My aunt turned, looking pink and confused. 'Ah, there you are, Nicola. This is Mr Delaney. He has been telling me he was delayed by business in London, just when we thought he wouldn't——' Her voice trailed away and she laughed self-consciously.

The dark-faced man nodded slightly and surveyed me with slow deliberation. I was conscious of the light that flooded through the windows and shone directly on my face, yet it was impossible for me to see the expression in the dark eyes that seemed to dissect me inch by inch. To my annoyance I felt colour creep into my cheeks. If this man thought he was going to reduce me to flustered incoherence, as he had Aunt Doris, he was very much mistaken, I told myself firmly.

'Do come and sit down,' Aunt Doris said fussily. 'You look so awkward standing there. What will Mr Delaney think of you?'

And it was important Rowan Delaney should approve of me, I thought bitterly, yet under his dark scrutiny I felt pallid and insignificant. The man had an overpowering arrogance that seemed to overshadow those about him and reduce them in stature. He gave the impression of belonging to another age. It was easy to imagine him in buckskin breeches and tiered cape, when in fact he wore well-cut tweeds that hung casually from his shoulders.

'I'm anxious to return to Raheen as soon as possible,' he said, 'so if it's convenient, we'll set off immediately, Miss Fletcher.'

'You must call her Nicola,' Aunt Doris put in eagerly. 'After all, she's so young and there is the relationship—slight as it is,' she added with another of her nervous laughs.

So she was already minimizing the relationship in case this haughty man might resent it, I thought hotly.

He raised his eyebrows and surveyed me quizzically. 'Well, Nicola, are you ready for the road?'

'I haven't packed yet,' I said sulkily.

'Not packed?' my aunt shrilled. 'Really, Nicola, how could you be so inconsiderate? Go up at once and get your things together. It's too bad Mr Delaney should be kept waiting, just because of your thoughtlessness.'

I got slowly to my feet and again I felt myself under scrutiny.

'And just why do you resent me so bitterly, Nicola?' he asked curtly.

I started at the suddenness of the attack. 'Resent—resent you?' I stammered.

'Obviously! Otherwise you would have made some preparation for travelling, or do you intend to make the journey in a light cotton frock and sandals?'

So the keen eyes had inventoried my clothing, but then he was the type of man who would coolly assess a woman's points. Well, he certainly couldn't have much of an opinion of me, I thought defiantly, realizing that my efforts to tidy my hair hadn't been particularly successful.

I gazed at him levelly. 'You must remember, Mr Delaney, that I had no choice in the matter. My aunt made these arrangements.'

'Nicola,' my aunt moaned in agitation, 'how can you talk like that?'

'Rowan is the name,' he put in quietly. 'As your aunt pointed out, we're relations in a sort of way.'

'It's a relationship which I assume from your letter

you are not anxious to claim. Did you expect me to be bubbling over with excitement because you've at last condescended to "collect" me, as you put it?'

'Ah, so that rankled!' He appeared to be amused.

'I'm supposed to be honoured that you've agreed to take me under your roof,' I choked. 'Well, for your information, Mr Delaney——'

'Rowan,' he again put in gently.

'Row—Row—Rowan,' I stammered in rage, then realized too late that I had obeyed him in this small matter. 'I intend to earn my keep. I want no favours from the Delaneys, understand that.'

I was vaguely aware that my aunt was frantically signalling me to stop, but I was beyond discretion. 'I shall earn my own living and be mistress of my own fate.'

'I find your attitude surprising,' he said mockingly. 'Most women seem to like being taken care of—at least, that has been my experience.'

Yes, no doubt women fluttered eagerly about this dark, magnetically handsome man, but I wasn't going to be one of them.

He must have read my thoughts, for he studied me for a moment in silence, then said in his deep abrupt voice, 'I'm afraid I find your attitude towards me completely irrelevant. However, now that you have given me your considered views, perhaps you will do as your aunt asks and collect your things. I want to get back to Raheen as soon as possible, and I'm not a patient man, as no doubt you will discover in due time.' Then, as I struggled for words, he swung around and began to speak to my aunt.

I wasn't particularly aware of what he was saying—

some triviality about his journey. I stood digging my fingers into the palms of my hands as I surveyed his broad back in impotent rage. I was being brusquely dismissed from his presence as though I were a rather tiresome and precocious child, whom he no longer found amusing.

For a moment I considered refusing to go with him, coolly and with dignity to announce that nothing on earth would induce me to share his roof. Then I caught sight of Aunt Doris, eagerly prattling, garrulous with relief that the situation was being firmly handled and that I was at last being safely taken off her hands. I had visions of the scenes that would ensue should Rowan Delaney leave The Hollies without me. Joyce too would not be slow to change her attitude, for I was under no illusions concerning her recent show of friendship. She would bitterly resent her mother's plans being thwarted and having to endure the repining and complaints that Aunt Doris would undoubtedly indulge in. Refusing to accompany Rowan Delaney was a luxury I simply couldn't afford. I turned and almost ran from the room.

In my bedroom I pulled from a cupboard the old-fashioned leather suitcase I had brought with me when I first came to The Hollies after my parents' death and began to cram my clothes into it, trying to stifle the sobs that were half mortification, half misery that once again I was in search of a home.

There would be no welcome for me at Raheen Castle, I realized. Only some lingering clan loyalty, that was deeper and stronger than his inclinations, could have induced Rowan Delaney to agree to my aunt's plans for my future.

None of the clothes that I was bundling into the case were new. Beggars can't be choosers, my aunt had said. Almost since my first day at The Hollies I had worn Joyce's hand-me-downs, but her figure was slightly plump and her clothes hung on me loosely and without elegance. But it didn't matter now. It was fairly obvious that Rowan Delaney had been unfavourably impressed by my appearance. Not that I cared! In fact, I would derive a perverse delight in looking as unattractive as possible, for I had the feeling that it would annoy and irritate him.

I was snapping the case shut when Joyce sauntered in. For a moment she looked at my activities and smiled. 'So you're all set for the big adventure.' She sprawled on the bed and watched as I brushed my hair and applied lipstick. 'Aha, so he's not so old and fat, is he?' she said slyly.

'No, he happens to be remarkably handsome,' I replied evenly. 'Handsome and boorish and proud and insufferable!'

She opened her eyes wide. 'But this sounds interesting! I think I'd like to catch a glimpse of this ogre.' She slid from the bed and surveyed herself complacently in the mirror. Her closely fitting dress suited her colouring perfectly. She looked groomed and confident and I knew she was already visualizing her effect on Rowan Delaney.

Well, she should be quite to his taste, I thought acidly. She should pass that searching glance with flying colours!

She looked at me absently as I pulled on a hat. 'Oh no, Nicola, you're not going to wear that monstrosity, are you? It's simply ancient.'

'I most certainly am,' I said firmly, 'Firstly because it's the one that looks least awful on me, and secondly, because I'm not going to Raheen Castle as a guest.'

'Oh, stop sounding like a martyr!' she said irritably. 'It's not as if you're going to some dingy little hole-in-the-wall. I remember hearing Daddy speaking about it, although at the time I wasn't particularly interested. It seems it's set on the west coast of Ireland. It's frightfully romantic, with turrets and battlements. It's said that it's hundreds of years old, but the Delaneys have restored most of it.' She gazed at me speculatively. 'I don't remember Daddy mentioning how many members there are in the family.' She giggled suddenly and I knew what was passing in her mind.

Raheen Castle sounded cold and remote. Suppose, when I arrived there, I found myself alone and isolated with Rowan Delaney? I thought with sudden alarm.

I picked up my case and walked to the door. Not for worlds would I let Joyce see how her words had affected me.

She followed me downstairs enlarging facetiously on the idea, unaware that as far as I was concerned there was something too grim and dangerous about Rowan Delaney to make her fantasies particularly amusing.

When we reached the drawing-room silence lay between Rowan Delaney and my aunt. Her garrulousness had been stifled by his obvious lack of interest in her and her affairs. She sat, flustered and uneasy, fidgeting with the large pink pearl beads at her throat. Our entrance was obviously a relief: her face lit up as she saw Joyce.

'Joyce, my pet, this is Mr Delaney. I was telling him that you're going to be married very soon.'

Joyce's eyes were bright as they met his. She tilted her head to one side and I could see she was bent on impressing him. 'I do hope Mother hasn't been boring you with my affairs. You see, she's inclined to think everyone's as interested in my marriage as she is. I've been rather spoiled, I'm afraid,' she ended with studied naïveté.

For the first time I saw a faint smile hover at the corners of his strongly chiselled lips. 'So I can see!'

The words were ambiguous, but after a slight hesitation Joyce evidently decided to accept the remark as a compliment and this assurance encouraged her to tread on ground that even my aunt had had sense enough to steer clear of. 'Nicola and I have been wondering if you live alone at the Castle,' she began brightly. 'It sounds such a lonely and isolated sort of place!'

He glanced at me briefly and my face burned with mortification. He would imagine I have been eagerly discussing him with Joyce and this was the last thing I wanted him to think. A studied aloofness concerning him and his affairs was the impression I wanted to convey.

There was a short pause, then he said brusquely, 'I'm not married, Miss Rochford, if that has been the burning question, but don't trouble that pretty little head of yours about my affairs.'

Startled, Joyce blinked her eyes in dismay, then glanced appealingly at her mother.

'Won't you have tea before you go, Mr Delaney?' Aunt Doris gushed. 'It's quite early yet and you've a long journey before you.'

'Thank you, no. As I mentioned, I want to get back

to Raheen as soon as possible.' He picked up my case. 'And now, Nicola, if you'll say your adieus we'll be on our way.'

I could sense a growing irritation in the way his brows had gathered into a frown. He was the type of man, I surmised, who would feel like a fish out of water when separated from his native background. Apart from that, at Raheen he would no doubt be lord of all he surveyed, I thought acidly, with control of the lives of those around him. Well, he was due for a shock, I told myself snugly. I, for one, was not going to become one of his vassals!

Now that the moment for parting had come, Aunt Doris's face quivered with easy emotion. 'Take good care of her, Mr Delaney,' she said. 'We shall miss her dreadfully, I know. Shan't we, Joyce?'

Joyce nodded coolly. For some reason or other she was venting on me her resentment of Rowan Delaney's rudeness. 'Really, Mother, there's no necessity to make a scene. I'm quite sure Nicola will be well able to take care of herself: she's that sort of person.'

During these exchanges Rowan Delaney had stood at the door watching us quizzically.

I brushed my lips swiftly against my aunt's soft cheek. We had never really got on well together. I had suffered too much under her meannesses and petty ways, and I had found her snobbery and worship of the conventions exasperating. She took out her hand-kerchief and dabbed her eyes carefully. 'You'll write, won't you?'

'Yes, yes, of course, Aunt,' I said, but I knew I wouldn't, and as I turned away I met Rowan Delaney's disconcerting gaze and I realized he knew I had lied. I brushed past him as I walked swiftly out of the room, turning away my head so that he couldn't see that my eyes were full of tears.

Aunt Doris and Joyce stood in the door of The Hollies and waved as the car moved along the short drive and passed the dense bank of green holly which had given the house its name.

He did not speak as the car hummed along the main road. I felt a strange sensation of unreality. Could it really be true that I was to accompany this man across the Irish Sea to a remote house in the west of Ireland! I now knew that he had no wife, but I still didn't know if he had relations, or even, I thought a little wildly, prisoners languishing in the castle dungeons, yet it would be impossible to question him. I had seen how Joyce had winced under his sharp rebuke.

I studied his profile covertly: it was like a deeply etched granite relief, I decided, the eye-sockets shadowed and enigmatic, the mouth firm and unrelenting. Again I felt tears well up, tears of misery and self-pity: the instruments on the wide dashboard blurred and glittered as I slowly eased my hand into my pocket and pulled out a handkerchief.

'Why don't you have a good cry and get it over with?' he asked suddenly, his eyes still fixed on the road.

'Thanks,' I said stiffly, 'but I'm not crying.'

'Oh yes, you are. You're feeling extremely sorry for yourself, aren't you?'

I blew my nose resolutely and sat upright. 'And why shouldn't I?' The Hollies is the only home I've known since I was young.'

'Young?' He glanced at me briefly. 'You're not particularly ancient as it is.'

'I was a schoolgirl when I went to live with my aunt. She's the only relation I have.' For some reason or other I felt defensive about Aunt Doris, probably because I sensed he considered her silly and futile.

'And you've hated every moment of your stay there, haven't you? You've been a handmaid to that vacuous pretty cousin of yours and your aunt used you as a sort of superior servant. Stop trying to pull the wool over my eyes, Nicola. You're anxious to bolster your position because you're so desperately keen to have me think you're not altogether without a background.'

'It's not true,' I burst out. 'After all, Uncle Victor and Aunt Doris gave me a roof when I was alone in the world. I owe them loyalty.'

'You owe them nothing,' he said curtly, 'so stop lying to me, Nicola.'

'I'm not lying,' I said stubbornly.

'Oh yes, you are. It's as much a lie as your promise to write to your aunt. You've no intention of ever getting in touch with her again, isn't that so?'

I shook my head in frustration. He seemed to be inexorably beating down my defences and it was so important that I should keep a part of my life secret as a sort of bulwark against him. I must not reveal how utterly alone and defenceless and at the mercy of fate I felt.

With an exclamation he swung the car skilfully in a wide arc as a small sports car dashed from a side-road. His large hands were strong and steady on the wheel: they were blunt-tipped and capable and somehow gave an impression of ruthlessness.

'For heaven's sake take off that ghastly hat,' he said

with sudden irritation. 'Are you deliberately trying to make yourself as unattractive as possible?'

I put up my hands and catching the brim rammed the hat further down on my head. 'I suppose,' I said coldly, 'it hasn't struck you that I'm satisfied with it?'

'Certainly not,' he said flatly. 'The hat has all the hallmarks of a hand-me-down—just as your coat has—and as probably most of your other clothes have. Cousin Joyce seems to have been generous with her cast-offs.'

I sat silent and overwhelmed with shame. But then he was the type of man who would observe every detail of a woman's apparel! I had been conscious of that searching regard from the first moment I had entered the drawing-room at The Hollies.

'Take it off,' he repeated curtly.

'I shan't,' I answered, and realized I sounded weak and querulous, like a defiant child.

'Look, Nicola,' he said, with an obvious effort to be patient, 'we're going to have a meal before the crossing, and I've no intention of having you look like a neglected waif.'

He was the type of man who would ordinarily be seen only with impeccably groomed and sophisticated women, I told myself, and wondered fleetingly if there was a particular woman in his life and if so what she looked like.

'If you dislike my appearance,' I replied stiffly, 'I'll wait in the car until you're finished.'

'You'll do nothing of the sort,' he answered evenly, 'and what's more, you won't be wearing that abominable hat.' And before I realized his intention, he took his left hand from the wheel and whisking the wretched hat none too gently from my head, pushed it into the glove compartment. 'You're really quite pretty,' he told me. 'There's no need for you to make a guy of yourself just to prove your independence. However, we can go into the subject of your clothes more fully when we reach Raheen.'

I sat in silence, appalled and outraged at the suddenness of his manoeuvre and the reference to his intentions when we reached Raheen. I tried to remain calm. Any show of anger would weaken my position and give him the advantage, I knew, and I had the depressing feeling that the situation was already slipping rapidly from between my fingers.

'I think it's time we reached an understanding,' I began with what dignity I could muster. 'You may as well know I've no intention of allowing you to dictate to me or interfere in my life in any way. If I go to Raheen it's on that understanding.'

We were approaching a country town and without answering he swung the car into the courtyard of a small hotel, then, switching off the engine, he turned and faced me directly. His deep-set eyes were hooded and gave me no clue to his mood, but there was about him an overpowering aura of leashed strength, and I realized even before he spoke that this battle at least was already lost.

'There's no "if" about it, Nicola: you're most certainly going to Raheen. Do you imagine for a moment that after taking you from the security—such as it was —of your aunt's home, and assuming responsibility for your future, I'm going to allow you to wander off on some hare-brained adventure, just because you happen to dislike me? Just remember that I'm completely in-

31

CHAPTER THREE

I AWOKE with a start to find my cheek pressed against the rough tweed cloth of Rowan's sleeve. For a moment I let it rest there, sleepily aware that we had been driving across Ireland for hours.

'So you're awake at last.' Rowan glanced down at me briefly.

I straightened with a jerk, wondering uncomfortably how long my head had been resting against his shoulder. I had fallen asleep as we drove between waving fields of ochre corn and lush green meadows dotted with cosy farms. Occasionally a hen would rush squawking across the road or a pinafored child would wave shyly from a cobbled yard. Now it was dusk and the scenery had changed dramatically. It was with a sense of shock I looked around at the thick fuchsia hedges that bordered the road. Beyond lay tiny stone-walled fields and patches of bogland pitted with sinister-looking dark pools. In the distance were jagged mountains over which a mist was beginning to drift.

A sudden unearthly screaming cry made me press against his shoulder in fright.

'It's only a curlew,' he said. 'They're very rarely seen, although one often hears them. It's from their uncanny cry that the legend of the banshee arose. However, I can assure you,' he added dryly, 'that the Delaneys have no banshee that wails on their demise, although certain other Irish families do claim that privilege.'

'I'd hardly call it a privilege,' I said.

'I expect you wouldn't,' he agreed, 'but then everything at Raheen will seem strange to you at first. However, time will rectify that and you'll become adjusted to what you will consider our peculiar ways and outlook—although it will take some time, I imagine.'

'As my stay under your roof will be very short, the question doesn't arise,' I told him coldly.

'What exactly are your plans, if I may ask?' He turned the car at a crossroads and ahead I caught a glimpse of sea: it looked dark and stormy and was ridged with white foam.

Detesting Rowan Delaney to the utmost, I had to admit to myself that I had made no plans, but on the spur of the moment I said acidly, 'I could look around. There's probably some kind of work I could do. There must be other families in this part of the country besides the Delaneys.'

'My dear girl, have you looked around you?' We were passing through a tiny hamlet and he nodded towards a group of small dejected-looking whitewashed cottages with broken roofs that clustered by the side of the road. 'Do you really imagine that the inhabitants of those cottages are in need of your services? Of course,' he went on musingly, 'there are the Fitzpatricks: they live in a big old ramshackle house, a few miles from Raheen. There are eight children, all of them horse-mad, who curse like troopers and whose last governess left with a nervous breakdown. Then there's Miss Bourke: she's a landscape artist and spends most of her time outdoors, and her leisure hours in the local pub. In fact there are several local

34

families I could name, but I'm afraid there are unsurmountable drawbacks in nearly every case.'

'Perhaps you could leave me to judge that for myself,' I said stiffly, 'or do you imagine yours is the only household without drawbacks?'

He gave a short laugh, but it was grim and humourless. 'Whether it is or not, you'll have to adjust yourself as best you can.'

His effrontery reduced me to silence and I was busily thinking up an answer when, in the distance, I caught my first view of the Castle. It stood high on a cliff-top and a pale moon outlined the towers and battlements while a slight mist shrouded the lower part of the building so that as we approached it appeared like a castle in a fairy-tale. In spite of myself I gave an exclamation of surprise and pleasure.

'Don't go romantic over Raheen,' he said abruptly. 'Distance lends enchantment. It can be bitterly cold here in winter. Terrific storms can blow up quite suddenly and the seas are treacherous.'

But perhaps by winter I should be gone, I thought. After all even Rowan Delaney, autocratic as he was, could hardly keep me against my wishes.

In spite of the long drive he showed no fatigue as we approached the tall iron-wrought gates. The dull glow of an oil-lamp lit up a small window in the low granite lodge and when he sounded the horn a man came out and began to unlock the gates: the moonlight was bright enough for me to see as he fumbled with the chains that he was short with slightly bowed legs and sandy hair.

As Rowan eased the car through the gates and drew up, he pushed his head through the window. 'It's good to see you back, sir,' he said with an air of heartiness which was belied by the small sly eyes that surveyed me curiously. 'And you've the young English lady with you too! Well, I'm afraid it's not much of a welcome you'll be getting up at the Castle. Doreen went and burnt her hand making the blackcurrant jam and is inside now putting on a poultice of bread-soda.' He nodded in the direction of the lodge. 'And Miss Ita's in a shocking temper or no doubt she'd have got something ready for ye. Such shenanigans as do be going on this evening was beyond everything.' He paused as though relishing the news. 'When I went up to fetch Doreen she was screaming her head off and Miss Ita was firing the pots and pans around, and her in a raging temper, and saying it wasn't her job to cook for the English girl.'

'I see,' Rowan said without inflection. 'Well, tell Doreen to take care of her hand and if she can't get up to the castle tomorrow I'll get one of the daily girls to substitute in the meanwhile. Goodnight, Thady.' It was a dismissal.

'Goodnight, sir.' Thady sounded flattened as he turned back and walked towards the lodge as though disappointed that his news had not caused some more interesting reaction from his employer.

We drove along a curving avenue, on each side of which were dark banks of shrubs. When at last the Castle loomed up I realized that I had indeed been romanticizing it. At close quarters it looked as grim and forbidding as its owner, the long mullioned windows gleaming coldly and unwelcomingly in the moonlight. I hesitated, reluctant to get out of the car. The journey had been long and tiring and the knowledge that I was travelling towards the unknown with this stranger had made me nervous and apprehensive. I was aware that my hair hung limply, and the realization that I looked drawn and exhausted didn't add to my self-confidence.

'Well?' His voice was a query. 'Are you getting out, or do you expect me to carry you over the threshold?'

The knowledge that he was quite capable of doing so made me quicken my steps.

In silence he pushed open the tall double doors and we entered the hall. A log fire glimmered in a huge stone fireplace and cast shadows on the high arched ceiling. At the opposite end of the hall a double staircase swept up towards a great mullioned window, then branched off on either side to long galleries. Thick sheepskin rugs were scattered on the slated floor and in spite of the fire I felt a sudden chill. Somehow the antiquity of the place made me feel an intruder, uncomfortable and ill at ease.

Then I saw a light appearing along one of the galleries and a girl holding an oil-lamp with a ruby shade moved forward. She paused for a moment at the top of the stairs, then almost reluctantly began to descend. Her long black hair fell to her shoulders and her skin was faintly tinted by the rosy light from the lamp. I knew immediately that she was Rowan's sister: she had the same severe classical features, but in her case they were subtly moulded into softly feminine lines. As she approached I could feel the atmosphere between brother and sister almost bristle with antagonism.

'I should have thought, as hostess, you would have had a meal prepared for our guest,' Rowan began tightly.

Without answering, the girl raised her lamp and re-garded me closely. 'So this is Nicola! Well, I'm not surprised, brother dear, that you're taking such an in-terest in her welfare. She's mighty pretty, although hardly up to Emer's standard.'

'May I introduce you to my sister Ita, who I regret to say prides herself on her atrocious manners,' Rowan said dryly.

'Doreen burned herself,' the girl replied sulkily, 'and you know how I hate cooking.' She paused a mo-ment, then said, as though conferring a favour, 'But I'll show her to her room if you like.'

'Don't bother,' Rowan said curtly. 'As you appar-ently don't intend to fulfil your duties as hostess, I'll do that myself.'

The girl shrugged indifferently. As she turned the light caught the other side of her face and with a sense of shock I saw that a scar puckered the corner of her lips: a small imperfection, yet it spoiled the perfect symmetry of her beauty. I glanced away quickly, but I was not swift enough.

'Don't bother to avert your eyes.' She sounded angry and challenging. 'I'm quite used by now to people's reaction. After all, I should be, shouldn't I, Rowan?' The glance she directed at her brother was full of venom and although he regarded his sister dispassion-ately I guessed that in some way or other her words had penetrated his armour. She turned and ran back up the stairs and I saw the shadow of her tall lithe figure as she disappeared along the gallery.

For a moment Rowan stood in frowning silence and I was aware he had forgotten my presence: crossing to the fire he kicked it into a blaze, watching abstractedly as the logs showered tiny crimson sparks up the enormous chimney. Then, with an effort, he seemed to direct his attention on me, as I stood self-consciously in the centre of the hall, not quite sure what was expected of me. I was tired and hungry and all the wind seemed to have been taken out of my sails by Ita's churlish reception. He offered no explanation of his sister's behaviour, however, and this didn't surprise me. It was typical of Rowan Delaney, I told myself resentfully.

'You're tired and hungry, I expect,' he said at last. With his back to the fire he regarded me, still with that look of frowning abstraction, as though I presented a tiresome and irritating problem. 'I'll show you up to your bedroom, then see if I can rustle something up in the kitchen.'

Immediately my pride, which had been dormant due to fatigue and the strangeness of my surroundings, flared up. 'Thanks,' I said tightly, 'I'd be glad if you'd show me to my room, but don't trouble yourself further concerning me.'

A sudden explosion of sparks, like a miniature fireworks, outlined his towering figure and brawny shoulders. He was a man who would always dominate his surroundings, I realized, whether it be Aunt Doris's drawing-room or the great hall of Raheen Castle. 'Don't be such a little fool,' he said shortly. 'You look completely exhausted and badly in need of some refreshment, or are you so keen to make a martyr of yourself and prove me a monster that you'd rather do

'You can hardly expect me to feel gratitude for the without?'

way your sister received me,' I said haughtily.

He looked faintly irritated, as though I had brought up an unpleasant incident that he had already disposed of. 'I'm afraid you'll have to learn to adapt yourself to our ways. I agree Ita is much too ready to take offence. At the same time,' he added dryly, 'I should imagine you're well able to defend yourself.'

He took up an ornate green and white glazed lamp from a table inlaid with a variety of coloured marbles and together we moved up the broad stairway. 'I'll show you to your room, then fetch something from the kitchens. Doreen probably left out something cold in spite of her accident. Unlike my sister, she tries to fulfil her duties, and I've the feeling that you've made up your mind to be worthy of your keep.' He was mocking me, I felt, and without answering I nodded rather grandly, though I had the feeling the gesture was completely lost on him.

At the top of the stairs he turned down one of the long galleries and as we passed the light caught the dull gilt of framed portraits, most of which were darkly toned and yellowed with varnish. It was impossible not to know that these were Rowan's forebears: the men had the same imperious deep-set eyes and arrogant carriage, whether they were dressed in doublet and hose or the dark respectability of frock-coat.

I slowed my steps as the lamp gleamed on a massive canvas of a man dressed in the fashions of olden days. He stood resplendent in a tall buckled hat and frilled cravat a tiered cape thrown back from one shoulder, his broad-fingered hands negligently toying with a quizzing glass. The likeness to Rowan was so striking that I paused, and Rowan, turning and seeing my attention on it, uttered an abrupt sound that might have passed for amusement.

'For heaven's sakes don't tell me how like I am to the fellow! He was one of our more disreputable forebears. He spent most of his time in England, where he was noted for his extravagances and on more than one occasion was accused of cheating at cards. Apart from that it's rumoured that when he ran out of funds he took to the road and became one of the most ruthless highwaymen of his time: in fact his exploits earned for him the title of the Black Delaney.'

Glancing more closely at the portrait, I thought I detected a cruel gleam in the eyes that seemed to stare sardonically into mine. As I turned away, uncomfortably aware that the features of the man by my side resembled those of his notorious ancestor in almost every detail, I got the impression that he was aware of my unease and was faintly amused by it.

At the end of the gallery we passed into a corridor. Halfway down he opened a tall oaken door and crossing to a bronze lamp that hung from the centre of the room, removed the glass chimney and put a match to the wick. 'We have only oil at present, but there are plans to bring electricity to the village. In the meanwhile you can regard the inconveniences as part of the old-world atmosphere!' But his very way of expressing himself took away any hint of apology his words might have conveyed.

I looked around with interest. It was an extremely large room with a high stuccoed ceiling depicting flying cupids and garlands of fruit and flowers. The furniture was dark and richly carved and the broad

41

bed had a headboard that reached halfway to the ceiling and was padded in petit point tapestry showing garlands of roses in faded tints of umber and old gold. A log fire blazed in the green marble fireplace and cast a warm light on the vast room. At least as far as my room was concerned the inhabitants of Raheen Castle had made some preparations for my arrival.

'I'll bring you something to eat,' Rowan said. 'Meanwhile you can get into bed, you look completely exhausted.'

'Thank you,' I said coldly, 'but I think I'll have it by the fire.'

'Just as you like,' he said indifferently.

When he had gone I glanced longingly at the wide comfortable-looking bed. I was weary and exhausted from the long drive across Ireland and the strain of being constantly on the defensive against Rowan. There was nothing I would have liked better than to slip between the snowy linen sheets that were turned down so invitingly, but I had no intention of doing so until Rowan had finally departed for the night, for I knew that once in the centre of that vast bed I would appear diminished and vulnerable, making it difficult for me to appear dignified and in command of the situation.

However, I decided to make a concession to comfort. Rowan had put my case on a richly carved chest with iron hasps placed at the foot of the bed, and I was aware how travel-worn it made my old leather case look as I took out a negligée of apricot silk with ruchings of a deeper tone of the same colour at throat and wrists. It was very beautiful and as Joyce had given it to me in the first triumphant flush of her engagement to Geoffrey this was something which for once had not been bestowed on me because it was too shabby for her own use. It suited my colouring and when I stood in front of the long mirror set in the centre panel of the enormous wardrobe I realized that, with my cheeks faintly flushed from the heat of the fire, I looked very pretty and not a bit as fierce as I intended, yet I couldn't resist a glow of satisfaction when I saw the expression on Rowan's face when he returned with the tray.

I was seated in an armchair by the fire when he pushed open the door and hesitated for a moment regarding me in silence, before crossing the room, yet in that short time I had seen something leap to life in the dark enigmatic eyes that made my heart beat in a little flurry of dismay and confusion.

I avoided his glance as he placed the tray on a small table by my side, but when I looked up at him again there was no sign of the look that had been strange and almost frighteningly aware.

Instead, he said sardonically, 'So you haven't taken my advice? However, you've managed to make yourself look very charming in that get-up, as no doubt you're well aware.'

'Thanks,' I said sharply, annoyed at the insinuation that I had changed into the negligée for his benefit, 'but I'm not in the least interested in your opinion of me.'

'Indeed?' He raised his eyebrows. 'So that extremely provocative garment was not intended to impress? Is that what you mean? Strange, for I always understood that most women dress solely for the benefit of the opposite sex.'

'Well, I'm not one of them,' I snapped.

He leaned back against the mantelpiece for a moment and regarded me thoughtfully. 'No, it would appear that in your own way Nicola, you are unique. But may I point out that you have very little cause for vanity? You're much too thin for one thing, although that can be rectified now that you're here at Raheen. Apparently, apart from overworking you, your relations have starved you as well.'

'It's natural for me to be thin,' I said. I was annoyed to find I sounded defensive and that he was subtly putting me in the position of being an unwanted waif dependent on his bounty.

'Nevertheless, you must eat up. At Raheen we don't encourage people to pick at their food. The Delaneys are a strong race who believe in living life to the full: they live hard and have, on occasion, died hard.'

'So I believe——' I began acidly. I stopped as I remembered Aunt Doris's account of the Delaneys: 'womanizers' and 'lawless' were the words she had used about them.

'I can see that your estimable aunt hasn't spared you where our history is concerned,' he said dryly. 'In that case, very little should surprise you while you're under the roof of the Delaneys. At least you won't be able to plead ignorance.'

As I uneasily digested this remark, he crossed to the door, then paused for a moment on the threshold. 'By the way, if I were you, I'd lock my door tonight.' But it was more a command than a request.

Anger at his tone made me say bluntly, 'And just whom should I lock it against? You, for instance?' The words rang out loudly and immediately I appalled as I

44

realized what I had said. It was impossible to read his expression from where I sat, but I got an impression of grim amusement.

'You don't mince your words, do you, Nicola? You know I'm beginning to think you have no *gradh* for me.'

I hesitated, wondering if he had used a Gaelic word deliberately to trap me into an indiscreet question.

'*Gradh* means liking, not loving, as you so obviously feared!'

'I didn't fear anything of the sort,' I blustered.

'Oh yes, you did. Actually, you're scared stiff of Raheen and the Delaneys, and in a way you may have good cause to be.' He paused for a moment before shutting the door behind him. 'By the way, I want to see you tomorrow before I leave the Castle. Come to my office immediately after breakfast. Doreen will show you the way.' There was no pretence that this was a request. It was a command pure and simple and as though to emphasize it he closed the door firmly behind him.

When he had gone I gazed with dismay at the tray he had set before me. An enormous portion of chicken and salad and wedges of obviously home-baked seed-cake were accompanied by a glass of rich creamy milk. I remembered seeing the shady outlines of cattle in a pasture as we drove up the avenue and I wondered if farming were the occupation that would take Rowan from the castle on the following morning. Then I remembered his peremptory instructions to see him in his office and hacked furiously at a roll to relieve my feelings. I was more hungry than I had realized, for I had almost finished the chicken and salad and had made inroads on the seedcake before I finally pushed the table aside.

The fire had died down and a red glow pulsed through the grey filmy wood ash, so that it trembled like particles of misty chiffon in the draught from the chimney. The light from the bronze lamp was sombre and I became uneasily aware of the shadows that loomed about the massive furniture and in the corners of the room. A wind had sprung up and I could hear it moan with slow uncanny insistence about some corner of the castle. I must turn the wick of the lamp up, I told myself, although I hadn't much hope it would ever illuminate the vast room.

I remembered the cruel face that had stared at me so hypnotically from the canvas in the gallery. Did the restless shade of the Black Delaney pace the corridors of Raheen Castle and I had the feeling that should they be certain that it did, the knowledge would not particularly disturb either Ita or her brother. Rowan was too like his notorious ancestor not to have inherited some of his traits. I remembered uneasily the strange dark look I had surprised on his face that night and his air of leashed strength and in spite of my determination to resist the danger of coming under his domination by unquestioningly obeying his commands I decided to lock my door. But I was tired and emotionally drained and the fire was a warm glow about my legs and, too lazy to move, I lay back in the armchair and let my mind drift aimlessly.

Suddenly the door crashed open and I started up with an exclamation of alarm as I regarded the tall lithe figure with the high cheekbones and brilliant slightly slanted black eyes who stood regarding me from the doorway. Without speaking he advanced into the room with the easy swinging stride that I had noticed in Rowan. He was dressed in mud-stained breeches and riding boots and a white shirt and he was openly laughing at my alarm. Nonchalantly he straddled a chair and folding his arms over the back regarded me, his dark eyes sparkling with interest and amusement.

I thought it time to show him I resented the intrusion. 'I haven't the remotest idea who you are,' I said icily, 'and I'd be obliged if you'd go.'

'Sorry to be disobliging, my poppet,' he said brightly, 'but I have no intention of letting the dawn rise without viewing the latest addition to Raheen. May I say you fulfil my fondest hopes; quite delectable, in fact, although if I were you I shouldn't have troubled getting into the negligée. The Delaneys don't necessarily need their women adorned, especially when they're pretty. We're a hot-blooded family and there's no one in a better position to inform you of this, as I happen to be Derry, Rowan's much-unloved brother.'

I gazed at him distrustfully. Apart from the dark, almost swarthy skin there was no real resemblance between this man and Rowan: the flash of white teeth in the hollow high-boned cheeks and the reckless vitality in the slanted eyes bore no resemblance to Rowan's brooding handsomeness.

'Oh, I know Rowan and I don't resemble each other, and there are lots of ways in which we differ, as you'll shortly discover.' He leaned over, removed a drumstick from the tray and chewed on it, still regarding me with bright-eyed interest. 'They say we're relations of a sort. Is that true?'

'So I'm told, but the relationship is very far out.'

'And the further out the better, as far as you're concerned, is that it, for I get the strong impression that you disapprove of us.'

In spite of his insolent disregard of the conventions I felt more at ease with Derry than I had with his brother. It was obvious he believed in saying exactly what passed in his mind and his lack of reserve was somehow reassuring.

He had finished gnawing on the bone and waved it warningly in my direction. 'If I were in your shoes I'd pack my traps and depart at the crack of dawn. I don't see you fitting in here and I really fear for you when Emer gets wind of your arrival: she's a pure hellcat when aroused.'

'Why should Emer, whoever she is, object to me when we haven't even met?' I asked curiously.

'Because, my poor dear innocent, Emer Lacey happens to be a redheaded devil who's set her crazy little heart on Rowan and doesn't believe in competition. Not, mind you, that I think you'd offer the least danger to her plans.' He tossed the bone into the fire and wiped his hands carefully on a handkerchief.

'Oh!' For some reason or other I felt deflated by this pronouncement.

'No, I don't seriously consider you in the running, for you're a prim proper well-bred young lady. Emer, on the other hand, has been brought up—if you could call it that—by her father, who's a hard-drinking horse-trainer and who has treated her like the son he always wanted. His idea of a sound education was to have her knocking around the stables since she was a kid, holding her own with his lads.'

'I can't see what possible difference it makes to me, for I can assure you I haven't the smallest interest in your brother's affairs.'

'But he obviously has in yours, otherwise he'd hardly have taken the trouble of lugging you over here!'

'You talk as if I'd no choice in the matter,' I said angrily. 'I can always leave Raheen if I choose. I assure you,' I added haughtily, 'that even someone as arrogant and self-opinionated as your brother would hardly keep me against my will.'

'I shouldn't be too sure of that if I were you. At Raheen Rowan's word is law. He owns a couple of copper mines hereabouts and believes in holding a sort of feudal control over all he surveys! I should know.' For a moment Derry's face lost its animation. 'He's arranged it that I work as a sort of superviser at the mines when I loathe the very sight of the place.'

'Then why don't you leave? Surely you could get fixed up somewhere else?'

He shook his head. 'It's as I told you. Rowan has only to drop a hint and no one will touch me with a ten-yard pole. I suppose I could head for a different part of the world, but it so happens that Raheen suits my particular needs down to the ground: there's good hunting and lots of pretty, willing wenches in the village, and plenty of convivial company when I feel in the mood for that sort of thing.'

'But he's a domineering bully,' I said hotly, 'and I, for one, don't intend to let him interfere in the smallest way with my life.'

Again the slanted eyes sparkled with amusement. 'This sounds interesting. I'll be fascinated to see how you fare if it comes to a head-on clash of wills,

49

although frankly, my dear little kinswoman, I wouldn't say you stood a chance!' He swung his leg over the chair and stood up. 'By the way, considering the relationship, don't you think a goodnight kiss would be in order?' As he spoke he advanced purposefully towards me.

I jumped to my feet, putting the armchair between us. 'I most certainly don't,' I said hastily, 'and now will you please go. It's late and I'm tired.'

He shrugged and turned away. 'Just as I thought, you're much too ladylike for this establishment!' But I could see that my refusal had merely pricked his interest. He was used to easy conquests and he was fully confident that in time he would overcome my defences.

When he was gone I crossed the room and locked the door, then before getting into bed I pulled back the long curtains at one of the windows and looked out. To the right a part of the Castle jutted out at an angle and through a lighted window on the ground floor beside a narrow door I could vaguely discern the figure of a man seated at a desk. This would be Rowan's office, I guessed, and for a moment I wondered what he wished to see me about on the following morning. Then I let the curtain drop, angry with myself for being interested in his intentions, especially as I intended to resist him in every possible way I could.

I turned out the lamp and lay for a long time in the dark, listening to the soughing of the wind and the hissing sound of the sea. I could hear the tiny creaks and sighs common to all old houses. The knowledge of the lamplight that burned in Rowan's office was vaguely comforting, and at last I fell asleep.

I awoke to the knowledge that some strange sound

had disturbed me. I hadn't been asleep long, I guessed, for moonlight still streamed through my window cutting a silver swathe across the floor. Then I heard it again—the faint drum of hoofbeats borne on the wind. As the sound drew nearer I got out of bed and crossed to the window. The lamplight still glowed in that ground-floor and the moonlight flooded the avenue, yet even though the hoofbeats pounded nearer and nearer, I could still see no sign of the approaching rider because of the banking evergreens that bordered the avenue. Whoever it was was coming at a tremendous pace, and I wondered why Rowan was showing no signs of curiosity. His figure was still to be seen at the table outlined by the mellow glow of the lamp.

Then quite suddenly a horse came into view ridden so furiously that as it swerved wildly around the curve and was abruptly reined in beneath the window, it reared back and almost crashed to the ground. To my amazement it was a girl who sprang from the saddle and in the brilliant moonlight I was able to see clearly that she had rippling red-bronze hair that hung to her shoulders and a pale heart-shaped face. From where I stood I could see that she was very beautiful, although her face was pinched and contorted with anger.

For a moment she stared up at the Castle as though undecided as to her next move then, catching sight of the light in the office window, she ran towards the door and hammered on it furiously with her riding crop.

I watched curiously wondering what Rowan's reaction would be to this invasion. He raised his head for a moment at the sound of the blows that rained on the door, then calmly seemed to resume whatever work

51

he was engaged in. I could see the girl almost dancing with impatience as she waited for the door to be opened, then, as it became obvious that she was to be ignored, she rained a further volley of blows on the panels. This then was Emer Lacey, the redheaded hellcat whom Derry had spoken of: both her behaviour and Rowan's reaction to her assault left me in no doubt. Once again the girl waited, having apparently exhausted herself. Then slowly Rowan got to his feet and crossed the room. I lost sight of him as he passed out of view for a few moments, then the door opened and I could see his tall broad figure filling the entrance.

Through my window which was slightly open at the top I could hear Emer say shrilly, 'What the blazes do you mean, Rowan Delaney, leaving me standing on the doorstep like a tinker?'

'Possibly because you're behaving like one,' he replied coolly. 'You seem to forget that I'm not at your beck and call, like your other male friends. Now will you kindly get back on that unfortunate animal of yours and return to Drumbeg, and let me get back to the accounts. You seem to forget I've my living to earn. Anyway, it's all hours of the night, and what's your father going to think if he finds you out riding hell for leather to Raheen?'

'Daddy's at the Curragh, and even if he weren't, you know very well I can twist him round my little finger, so don't fob me off with that stuff, Rowan Delaney!' Her voice quivered with rage.

'All right, then.' Rowan sounded faintly weary. 'Let's consider your reputation. What are the villagers going to think when they hear you pounding up to the Castle at this hour of the night? Naturally they'll assume the worst. I do wish, Emer, you'd try and show a little sense and not act on impulse. Apart from that, these displays don't impress me in the slightest—and incidentally, I'm at a loss to know what this particular visitation is in aid of.'

'You know perfectly well, so you needn't stand there doing the holier-than-thou act. I've heard you brought a girl back from England and you didn't even have the decency to tell me yourself. I had to hear it from Derry —of all people. He announced it down at Reilly's pub in front of a crowd of people. You can imagine the way he made it sound.'

'I can imagine,' Rowan replied dryly.

'No, you can't,' she replied, her voice quivering as though she were close to tears of anger and frustration. 'He made it sound as if you were starting up a harem or something, in the Delaney tradition.'

'I can't really see why the sins of my forebears should be visited on me,' Rowan said, then added abruptly as though he were fast losing patience, 'and anyway, Emer, it's really none of your business whom I bring back to Raheen.'

'Who is she?' Emer asked with feverish intensity. 'What does she look like? Is she young, old? People have linked our names together whether you like it or not: I've a right to know.'

'You've no right in the world,' he said shortly. 'However, as you've taken so much trouble to obtain what you evidently consider vital information, I'll do my best to satisfy your curiosity. Let's see, how would one describe Nicola Fletcher?' He paused consideringly and I guessed he was deliberately provoking her. 'She's thin—too thin, perhaps——'

'But what does she look like?' Emer interjected impatiently.

'Pretty! Not beautiful like you, Emer.'

'Oh!' I could almost hear the sigh of relief.

'But she has a strange unusual quality that's elusive and hard to place. It's something a man might find intriguing to investigate if he had a mind to.'

'So it was to give yourself ample time to investigate this—this—strange elusive quality that you brought her back to Raheen, under your very roof so that the whole district can have no doubt of your intentions?' Again her voice rose sharply.

'You forget she's a kinswoman of mine,' he said smoothly.

'That's only an excuse, Rowan Delaney. You've never cared a damn what became of your relations. Look at what you did to Ita——'

'Let's leave Ita out of this.' Suddenly his tone was savage.

The girl paused, as though reconsidering her tactics, then said almost provocatively, 'Aren't you going to ask me in for a drink, Rowan? I've a long ride back.'

'I'm going to do nothing of the sort. I've a good idea what you have in mind, but I'm not one of your puppets to be manipulated as you do any male whom you happen to fascinate. I've a built-in resistance to your beauty, Emer, so don't waste your time.' His voice was cutting, and I wondered if he were deliberately steeling himself to resist the allure that she seemed to be able to project at will.

At his words she winced back and I could see her white, perfectly proportioned face twist with hysterical rage. Then, with the swiftness of a snake, she raised

54

her riding crop and struck him viciously across the cheek, and for a moment I could almost feel the tension and violence that her action seemed to generate between them. Then he reached out and pulled her towards him and they were close in each other's arms. As their bodies merged with the shadows I turned away from the window.

CHAPTER FOUR

ON the following morning I awoke to the sound of someone tapping on the door. I jumped out of bed and turned the key and felt rather foolish when I saw that Ita was standing outside holding a small tray.

She looked at me in surprise, then said with the bluntness that was typical of the Delaneys, 'For heaven's sakes, why did you lock your door? Did you expect to be murdered in the night?'

I could hardly tell her that the Delaneys and Raheen Castle made me nervous and apprehensive, but to my relief she didn't wait for a reply but followed me into the room and placed the tray on the bedside table.

'I've brought you some tea and toast, as breakfast won't be till later, and anyway, it's a sort of peace-offering!' Then she added with a rush, 'I'm sorry I was so beastly to you last night, but Rowan always brings the worst out in me.'

I slipped back between the sheets and she crossed to the windows and began to pull back the curtains, letting the glowing light of early morning flood the room. She had lost some of the sullenness of the previous evening and, with her dark hair dressed in a high chignon, she looked maturer.

'Did you sleep well?' she asked indifferently. 'No one goes to bed early here, but then I expect you'll find us rather unconventional and slapdash in lots of ways. Rowan didn't condescend to tell me much about you, but if you're used to a well-regulated household you'll find this a bit hard to put up with!'

Remembering Aunt Doris's well-regulated household, I said, 'Well, I suppose my aunt was an orderly sort of person: meals were always served punctually and Joyce and I had certain set hours for our different occupations.'

'Joyce? Who is she?' For the first time she showed some real interest in my affairs.

'Joyce is my cousin. She's getting married soon.'

She sat down on the end of my bed and regarded me thoughtfully. 'And do you like her?' Her forthright manner somehow suited her dark sullen looks.

'Well——' I hesitated.

She shook her head impatiently. 'You can tell me, without beating about the bush. I either like a person or I don't, and I make no pretence about it.' As she saw my expression she put her hand to her mouth in sudden compunction. 'Oh dear, I'm being rude and beastly again!'

There was something so endearing about her contrition that I laughed and said, 'Well, no, I don't really like Joyce very much, but then I expect it's because we're so very different. There's hardly any subject we agree on.'

'Then you were glad to leave when Rowan came for you?'

I hesitated, remembering how I had loathed his proprietorial attitude and his careless assumption that I was to be disposed of according to his will. 'I had no choice in the matter. Aunt Doris is giving up her house when Joyce marries.'

'Because she doesn't want you?' she asked bluntly.

'Is that it?'

I nodded, and she regarded me sombrely.

'I expect if you'd had any choice in the matter you wouldn't have come here?'

'Well, I should certainly never have agreed to be flung on your brother's charity if I'd known beforehand that my aunt was planning to get in touch with him.'

'What would you have done?' she asked curiously.

'Oh,' I replied proudly, 'I'd probably have taken a job of some kind.' They were brave words, but I knew in my heart that Aunt Doris had been right: without training how could I have obtained decent employment?

'I can certainly understand your not wanting to go with Rowan. He's completely insufferable.' Her eyes darkened. 'Be careful of him and don't let him ruin your life as he has mine!'

I looked at her doubtfully, wondering if she were dramatizing herself as she stood up and began to wander restlessly about the room.

Then, with a rush, she said, 'It's Rowan's fault that I have this hideous scar. But for him I'd be married now with a home of my own, and as far away from him and Raheen as possible.'

The bitterness of her tone shocked me and for a moment I was at a loss for words, then I said hesitantly, not quite sure how she would take it, 'It's so small, Ita: not really as noticeable as you imagine! Don't you feel you're exaggerating things a little?'

She swung around fiercely. 'Oh, it's easy for you to talk, but I've seen how people look at me. You've no idea what it's like: their pitying expressions! I know just what they're saying about me, "So sad about the Delaney girl! She'd have been quite a beauty if it hadn't been for that accident on the rocks at Raheen——" ' She stopped and choked on a sob.

'Do come and sit down and tell me about it, won't you, Ita,' I said softly, for I had the feeling that this visit and what she called her peace-offering was an attempt to establish a friendship between us. It was obvious that her grievance against her brother had been building up and that she longed to pour out her troubles to another woman.

Reluctantly she stopped her restless pacing and sat down again on the side of the bed. 'I expect it all really began when our parents died. Rowan, as the eldest, took over the management of Raheen and the mines. I was away at school at the time and it wasn't until I returned home to live that I realized I was trapped here and that unless I fought for a life of my own I'd never be free of Raheen.'

'Trapped?' I asked uneasily.

'Yes, trapped,' she repeated fiercely. 'Oh, he gave a ball for me, saw I had the right clothes, and did all the right things: he even made sure I met what he considered eligible men! But when I really fell in love it was a different matter.' She paused broodingly and then said in a rush, 'I met Brian Carbery last year: he's an archaeologist and was working on a tumulus a few miles inland. He's older than I am and completely different from me in every way: I suppose that's what attracted me to him in the first place. He was everything I ever wanted in a man I would marry: gentle and kind and sensitive! The type of man Rowan could never understand! When I told him we planned to

59

marry, he was furious. You see, he still considers me a child: his schoolgirl sister with a crush on a brilliant man much older than herself, who was taking advantage of her naïveté.' She paused and looked at me appealingly. 'But it wasn't like that really. Oh, I know Brian's more experienced than I am, and hasn't much money and a completely different background, but these things don't count with me.'

'But they count with Rowan!' I said. Everything she was telling me fitted with my own conception of the man.

She nodded. 'Brian was perfectly straightforward from the start. He called on Rowan and explained everything, but Rowan wouldn't even listen. He treated Brian as if he were an insolent upstart and made it plain he considered he had taken advantage of a silly infatuated school-child. Afterwards he did everything in his power to prevent us meeting, but we met in secret. Brian hated the subterfuge, for in his own way, he's every bit as proud as Rowan, but I think Rowan had convinced him that he was being unfair to me. He became terribly conscious of the difference in our ages and began to get it firmly fixed in his mind that he was ruining my life. I could see my only chance of happines slipping between my fingers and in desperation I suggested we go off together secretly. Of course I could have had a good row with Rowan and simply marched out, but I had no intention of facing another ghastly scene and apart from that——' She hesitated and then said almost shyly, 'And I suppose at that time the idea struck me as daring and romantic!'

She stopped and I said, 'He found some way of preventing you, of course.'

She did not reply, but her fingers moved to the left side of her mouth and touched the scar. 'It was then I got this!' Her voice rang out in bitter protest.

'But how——' I began.

'Does it matter? It's happened, that's all that counts.' Her eyes darkened. 'Brian insists it doesn't make any difference, but then he would: he's that type of man, but I'm not going to let him marry me out of pity. He has frightfully high standards about everything, and is a perfectionist, and sometimes when I'm angry or upset it's frightfully noticeable.'

As she spoke she turned her head and I noticed in the brilliant light that it was a crimson weal against the pallor of her face 'You see,' she said bitterly, 'you met me in lamplight, and that's always considered to be flattering to a woman and, whether I like it or not, I'm too much of a Delaney to take pity from anyone— even Brian! I'd say cruel wounding things that would end anything that was ever between us.'

I could see it would be hopeless to reason with her or even to suggest that surgery might solve her problem, for I had the feeling she might consider it an intrusion and our friendship wasn't well enough established for me to risk a rebuff at this stage.

She stood up suddenly and I could see she was already regretting her urge to confide.

'Shall I have time to have a walk before breakfast?' I asked.

She nodded. 'Doreen sent up word that she's not coming up today and it will mean I'll have to do the cooking. I hate domestic work and I'm no good at it, so meals will be late until Doreen returns, but at any rate I'm not as handless as the daily girls who do nothing but gossip and giggle and flirt with the yard men. If you'd like to go for a swim I'll lend you togs; that's if you haven't brought any of your own.'

I smiled and shook my head. 'I didn't know sea-bathing was part of the programme at Raheen.'

Her eyes brightened and I guessed that the sea was one of her rare enthusiasms. 'Oh yes, and we've a stretch of private beach. It's a sort of cove, just below the cliffs, but be careful of the tides about Raheen Point: it can be dangerous there, especially at this time of the year.'

'I don't feel a bit adventurous: I'll stick to the cove, I think.'

'Then I'll leave the togs in the hall and you can collect them on your way out. There's a small cave cut into the cliff that's perfect for changing in.'

When she had gone, I dressed quickly, feeling my spirits rise. The sun spilled through the windows and the room, instead of looking dark and threatening as it had on the previous night, seemed simply to hold the mellowness of age.

The hall was deserted when I collected the bathing things that Ita had left on a table. I stood for a moment outside the door. On all sides the castle seemed to rear up precipitously. I could smell the salty tang of the sea, but had no idea how to reach the cove. Then to the left through an archway I caught a glimpse of a cobbled courtyard. I walked towards it. Perhaps Thady or some of his minions would be around and would direct me! Outbuildings lined three sides of the yard and a row of milk churns stood outside a byre. The morning's work was evidently already finished and a boy was half-heartedly sweeping between the stalls. When I looked in he stopped and gaped at me, and when I asked him the way to the beach he shook his head vacantly and pointed across the yard to the stables.

'Old Thady's in there, looking for eggs, along o' Bernie.' He sniggered. 'You'd think he was old enough to know better, wouldn't you?'

Not quite knowing how to reply to this remark, I headed for the stables, and as I approached a young girl in a red flowered apron burst out of the doorway and rushed past me, screaming with laughter. 'You ought to be ashamed of yourself, Thady Keating,' she called shrilly over her shoulder, 'and if Doreen was here I'd tell her this minute the way you're carrying on when her back is turned!' Then, with a surprised glance in my direction, she scuttled out of sight.

When I went in, Thady appeared to be industriously searching in a horse's crib filled with straw, but there was an unmistakable gleam in his small sly eyes. He was not as old as I had thought him to be on the previous evening and I guessed from his wizened appearance that he had been a jockey in his youth. He was, at any rate, apparently taking full advantage of his wife's accident to dally with the daily girls.

'Ah, there you be, up bright and early, like myself! I do be looking for eggs,' he explained. 'There's an old Rhode Island hen that lays hereabouts and I'm partial to a brown egg. Take no notice of young Bernie, miss,' he said virtuously. 'She's a terror for pestering a man. Man-mad, that's what I calls her. If Doreen was here today she'd soon knock some of the nonsense out of that one. But poor soul, she's poorly, what with her hand being bad and her nerves not up to much. Miss

Ita won't like doing the cooking, no doubt, but she's lucky anyone at all will come up to the Castle, it being the way it is.' He sucked on a straw and regarded me expectantly, evidently hoping I'd show interest in this ambiguous statement.

I felt curious, but not for worlds would I question him about affairs at Raheen, for I was certain if I did so it would come to Rowan's ears. 'The Castle's very big, of course,' I said cautiously. 'It must be difficult to get staff.'

''Tisn't as simple as that, miss! The Castle has a bad name hereabouts. 'Tis said,' he lowered his voice, 'that it's haunted.'

'Haunted?' I exclaimed, and he had the satisfaction of seeing that this information had shaken me badly.

'That it is! Sure why should I be coming up to collect Doreen every afternoon? She's scared out of her wits to walk down the avenue alone. It's there they say the Black Delaney gallops with his cloak flying behind him, like he did in the old days when he was out robbing and murdering people.'

I looked startled and he nodded with a satisfied air. 'Oh yes, indeed, the Delaneys had always a fierce bad name about these parts for their reckless devil-may-care ways. There's Master Derry behaving something shocking with the village lassies and Miss Ita making a show of herself last year, flinging herself at the Englishman's head, and as for Mr Rowan himself'—he put his head to one side and leered knowingly—'they say he's got the charm of the Black Delaney himself and that there's not a girl for miles around who wouldn't give her two eyes to be his bride and queen it here at Raheen Castle.'

'Would you tell me the way to the beach?' I asked hastily as I could see Thady was eagerly awaiting my reaction to this piece of information.

'Ah sure, I'm keeping you from your swim with all my chatter, amn't I, miss?' he said blandly. 'Well, you just go through that iron gate there set into the wall and walk down through the orchard and you'll come to a small wicket gate that lets out on to the cliff path.'

I followed his directions and went through a large orchard. Ruddy apples were thick on the low branches of old trees and against the walls I could see peach and pear trees.

Once outside the small wicket gate I came on a path of coarse tufted grass that bordered the cliff. Gulls swooped and screamed against the sky that was as translucent as blue silk and far out to sea I could make out the white billowing sails of a yacht. I followed the path until it branched off to a steep track clumped with the rose pink bells of escallonia that grew like a weed. The track twisted down to a sickle of fine sand bounded with rocky pools. I could see the sand gleam through the shallow waves that lapped the shore and as I scrambled down the cliffside I stumbled on a root, then recovered myself with a shudder of fear as I saw the jagged rocks beneath.

I found the cave easily enough in the tiny cove. It was small and charming with a floor of smooth sand as fine as sugar: dried seaweed dangled from its rocky sides and near the roof and I guessed that in winter the sea must lash up against the cliffside.

I swam out until I was able to get a comprehensive view of the cove. On one side I noticed that the rocks gave way to a sheer precipitous cliff that jutted out into the sea. About it the waters tumbled and boiled and I guessed, even from the distance, that it would be a dangerous spot for an inexperienced swimmer. This must be Raheen Point that Ita had warned me about and I determined to steer clear of it.

The water was icy cold and I didn't prolong my swim: I waded back to the cave and dressed quickly. As I made my way back to the cliff path I realized with a sense of shock that I was not alone in the cove. A thin scholarly-looking man with greying fair hair was leaning with his back against a rock, contentedly smoking a pipe. His blue eyes regarded me whimsically.

'You swim well, Miss Fletcher. Even better than Ita! She won't like that, as she's proud of her prowess.' He laughed almost gaily at my surprise that he knew my name. 'I assure you the whole district knows of your arrival, and you'd be surprised at the speculations that are buzzing around concerning you!'

I flushed as I remembered Thady's remarks concerning the Delaneys.

He noticed it and immediately the laughter left his eyes and he said gravely, 'I can assure you there was nothing snide meant in that remark! It's simply that we have so little to interest us here that a newcomer makes a refreshing change. Won't you sit down and chat with me for a few moments, Miss Fletcher? I've been here for hours with nothing but the seagulls to keep me company. May I introduce myself: I'm Brian Carbery and I'm by way of being an archaeologist. I was working on a dig up till now, but the rest of my party have gone home until next year and I'm left alone with the melancholy relics of another age. I often walk out here it makes a change of scene.'

Here too he would be close to Raheen Castle and Ita Delaney!

His blue eyes were penetrating and he must have guessed my thoughts. 'Does she ever speak of me?' he asked, almost shyly.

I hesitated, then, on impulse, said, 'She loves you very much. You must believe that.'

He nodded wryly. 'Yes, strangely enough I do.' He stopped and looked at me keenly. 'Did she tell you how she met with her accident?'

I shook my head. 'Only that you planned to marry and that Rowan ruined everything for her.'

He nodded and puffed reminiscently. 'We arranged to meet on the headlands and walk along the cliff path to my lodgings. The season was over and the English party I was working with were going home and we intended to return with them and get married in England. But somehow Rowan got wind of the plan. He followed her and she got into a panic. She had some wild idea that if we should meet Rowan would kill me. Anyway, she raced along the cliff path. It was dusk and she must have stumbled against a boulder.' He paused and his face darkened. 'She pitched headlong over the cliff. Fortunately some bushes broke her fall, otherwise she'd certainly have been killed. She was unconscious for days and afterwards there was left this scar on her mouth. Nothing will convince her that I don't give two hoots for what is after all a fairly minor blemish, and of course I can hardly suggest plastic surgery as it would only confirm her in her ideas about my attitude.' He sighed. 'It's rather a problem because much as she dislikes Rowan she has a lot of her brother in her: the same dark unrelenting pride, and I'm rather an easy-going sort of chap and my family are ordinary conventional law-abiding citizens. So you see I find the Delaneys rather hard to understand.' He knocked out his pipe against a rock. 'I feel rather guilty about bothering you with my problems. Anyway, it's time I was getting back. I'm brooding over some shards. It gives me a good excuse for hanging about this part of the country.'

'Shards?' I queried.

'Broken bits of pottery that were used about 2000 B.C.' His eyes lit with enthusiasm. 'If you're interested perhaps one day you'll call over and I'll show you around the dig. It can be very interesting even to those who don't know or care about archaeology.'

'Thanks, I'd love to, but I don't know the way. But perhaps Ita would show me,' I added mischievously.

He laughed a little guiltily. 'That's exactly what I hoped you'd say!'

We parted at the top of the cliff and I retraced my steps along the path. What I had heard only confirmed me in my original opinion of Rowan Delaney and his arrogant assumption of power over those around him. It was obvious that he already considered me as part of his household, a chattel to be directed and disposed of at his will, and I was determined to resist him to the utmost. In me he had found an antagonist who would fight tooth and nail for her independence.

It was only when I glanced at my watch that I realized with a shock how late it was. Breakfast must be long over now even if it had been as late as Ita had predicted. I ran the last part of the way, remembering uneasily that Rowan had demanded I see him in his office after breakfast. I was breathless as I raced around the front of the Castle: then I stopped short, my heart beating painfully with exertion and alarm for Rowen was pacing impatiently in front of the office wing and he looked furious. Now was the time to carry out my resolve. I swept back my hair and walked towards him, determined to appear coldly indifferent to his mood, and hoped that I didn't look too flustered and apprehensive.

'Do you realize that breakfast has been over for the last half hour?' he began curtly. 'I made it clear I wished to see you this morning.'

'I went for a swim and I didn't realize how late it was.' I was annoyed to find that in spite of myself a faint note of apology had crept into my voice.

'So I see!' He glanced at the damp bathing things under my arm. 'But it hardly accounts for the length of time you've been away, does it?'

Instantly anger flared up at his catechizing tone. This was the man whose fierce possessiveness had destroyed his sister's chance of happiness! Now was the time to put my foot down and show him exactly on what terms our future relationship was to be based.

'I wasn't aware you intended to time my actions,' I said furiously, 'otherwise I shouldn't have gone swimming in the first place!'

He regarded me without expression. 'You're perfectly free to come and go as you like, provided you try to conform to the ways of the household. As a rule I leave for the mines immediately after breakfast, and this delay is going to make me hopelessly late.'

'I understood from Ita that, on the whole, the Delaneys are an unconventional family and not given to keeping timetables,' I said bitingly. 'Perhaps you'd prefer to put our interview off to a more convenient time.'

There was a short silence and I could see he was surprised at what he considered my audacity. 'We'll do nothing of the sort. It's obvious the sooner we come to an understanding the better,' then added impatiently, 'and do stop acting like a silly little child, Nicola, for I can assure you it cuts no ice with me.'

If it had been his intention completely to rout me, he succeeded, for I blushed up to the roots of my hair at the unexpectedness of these tactics.

Without waiting to witness my confusion he ushered me into the office. It was a low-ceilinged room with walls completely panelled in dark glowing woods. Apart from a row of filing cabinets and a modern teak desk and chairs it was completely empty. He motioned me to take a chair, then stood for a moment gazing frowningly through the window. I got the impression that whatever he was going to say to me was not going to prove easy and the knowledge was balm to my wounded ego.

Then he turned and, to my surprise, said almost gently, 'When we first met, Nicola, you gave me the impression that you resented the prospect of living under my roof without earning your keep.'

I nodded. 'Naturally I didn't want to live on your charity.'

He regarded me with some of his old asperity. 'I could think of a happier way of putting it! However, as you're determined to be unpleasant I'll lay my cards on the table without any conversational frills. I want you to make friends with my sister. I know she's not an easy person to get on with and, to a certain extent, I'm responsible for that.' He paused and then went on as though with an effort, 'She has suffered a disappointment concerning plans she had made for her future and indirectly I was the cause of that scar which she is so conscious of and which she resents so bitterly.'

I waited silently, wondering if he were going to admit his part in putting between his sister and Brian Carbery. He sat down and leaned his elbows on the desk and I saw that his face was suddenly drawn and haggard.

'I want you to gain her confidence. Perhaps if she could speak to another woman it would help to take away that dreadful bitterness that's withering her up and destroying her happiness.'

'Her happiness was destroyed when you prevented her marrying the man she loved,' I blurted.

His face whitened. 'That's no concern of yours! I'm simply asking you to be a companion to Ita. As you're so keen to earn your living I'm offering you the opportunity. But only,' he added in measured tones, 'on condition that you don't encourage her in any way to get in contact with Brian Carbery!'

For a moment there flashed into my mind the picture I had witnessed from my window the previous evening, of Emer Lacey close in his arms. For himself there was perfect freedom to love whom he chose, but for those around him there was only the iron grip of a merciless dictator.

CHAPTER FIVE

I HAD opened my lips to tell him that I had no intention of obeying his arbitrary command when there was a loud knock on the door and Ita marched in. She looked at us briefly, then, ignoring her brother, said, 'I'll get you some breakfast, Nicola, if you come down to the kitchen—although I can't guarantee the cooking will be first class.'

There was a short pause and I waited uncomfortably. As Ita was making such a point of ignoring Rowan's presence I wasn't sure whether I should assume my interview with him had concluded and accompany his sister without further ado or whether I should wait for some intimation from him that I was free to go.

Ita turned impatiently towards the door. 'Well, are you coming, or are you waiting for your dismissal from the boss?'

I glanced at her in alarm—had she guessed that Rowan's appointment with me had closely concerned herself?—then bit my lip in mortification as I realized she was simply using me as a means of expressing enmity towards her brother.

He didn't deign to speak and awkwardly I followed her from the room.

As we walked towards the main wing she began to question me without any pretence of diplomacy of finesse. 'Well, what did he want to see you about? It must have been something pretty confidential or else he wouldn't have made a point of seeing you in his office. Actually I wouldn't need to ask you if he hadn't got the rooms in the office wing blocked off: at one time it was all part of the Castle and it was quite easy to hear all that went on by approaching it from the inside and standing in the passage.' She laughed without humour. 'Among other things I've heard some mighty interesting scenes between him and Emer: it used to make my blood boil to hear how rottenly he treated her. Anyway, I must have given myself away some time or other, for the next thing was he got a brick wall put up in jig time.'

I glanced at her, appalled at the casual way she had admitted to eavesdropping on her brother, and she had the grace to grin a little shamefacedly. 'Well, what else was I to do? Rowan doesn't let me know what's going on, and I've a right to know—especially when it concerns my own life.'

For a moment she was silent and I guessed her mind was on Brian Carbery and her brother's part in putting between them and his implacable determination that they should not resume their friendship.

She glanced at me in sudden suspicion. 'He wasn't talking to you about me, was he?' she asked fiercely. 'Because if he has any ideas of using you as a spy, to go running to him in case I get in touch with Brian, you're wasting your time.' She drew in her breath, as though she were holding back sobs, and then said without emphasis, 'I've no intention of ever meeting or seeing Brian again.' But I noticed that her eyes were bright with tears before she turned her head away in a proud little gesture that was somehow touching and poignant.

As I followed her to the kitchen quarters through long cold passages and gloomy rooms with slated floors and shelving I felt a warm sympathy for the girl and her broken life, and I had the feeling that in her own surly manner she had begun to extend a grudging friendship.

In contrast to the rooms surrounding it the kitchen was an enormous cheerful place with red-tiled floor and whitewashed walls, against which hung copper skillets and silver domed dish-covers which obviously hadn't been in use for many years. A white scrubbed table ran almost the full length of the room and on the great black range with red-hot bars various pots and pans simmered and boiled. At a stone trough into which ran water from a single brass tap Bernie, the little servant girl in the red floral apron, was washing breakfast dishes and singing in a loud hoarse voice.

'For goodness' sake, Bernie, must you make such a hideous noise?' Ita pushed her hair back and looked about her irritably. 'And now what have you done with the frying-pan?'

'Sure I put it away. Isn't the breakfast over long since?' Bernie returned defensively.

'Miss Fletcher hasn't had hers yet. Now fetch it, and don't take all day about it.'

Languidly the girl took her soapy hands out of the water, eyeing me with open curiosity. 'Thady was telling us you went down to the water afore breakfast,' she giggled delightedly. Evidently in the kitchen quarters my behaviour had been considered amusingly eccentric. As she slowly dried her hands in a thick roller-towel she studied every detail of my appearance with eager interest. 'Peggy was real disappointed not to get a look at you this morning when she went up with the breakfast. She's mad after the style, so she is.'

As I looked at her blankly she said, by way of explanation, 'Peggy's me cousin, and she works here too, and when she heard you was from England she knowed you'd have the latest fashions, for her mind's on nothing else from morning till night.'

Well, if Peggy was interested in fashion she'd hardly get much satisfaction from viewing the simple worn beige woollen dress I had put on that morning, I thought wryly.

Ita, who was rattling pots at the range, turned impatiently. 'Do fetch the frying-pan: I don't intend spending the entire day here.' As she spoke she pushed laboriously at a great oval pot that took up most of the centre of the range.

'Don't move the pigs' food, or Thady will be lighting: you know the way he do be about them pigs!' Bernie shrilled as she rummaged in a cavernous cupboard and, producing an enormous iron frying-pan, dumped it on the range with a clatter, adding coaxingly, 'Let me do Miss Fletcher's breakfast: I'm a great hand with the cooking.'

'You go upstairs and help Peggy with the rooms,' Ita said firmly, 'and tell her to pay more attention to the dusting. Mr Derry's room is a disgrace.'

'It's Mr Derry himself who's the cause of it all,' Bernie replied pertly. 'He's always flinging his things about every which way.'

Ita sighed as Bernie departed. 'I'm afraid I'm simply not the domesticated type or I'd have more control over the girls, but frankly, housekeeping bores me stiff.'

Would it have been a different matter if she had married Brian Carbery? I wondered. What was a wearisome chore at Raheen might have become a labour of love. I could well imagine Ita Delaney happily bustling about her own home, preparing for her husband's return.

For a moment I wondered if I should tell her of my encounter with Brian, then hesitated. I might be met with old reserve and this beginning of a friendship between us jeopardized.

'You found your way to the beach all right?' she asked idly as she spread a checked cloth at one end of the table, then with an exclamation rushed to the range and rescued the pan which was belching clouds of dark greasy smoke.

I nodded. 'I met Thady in the yard and he directed me.'

Immediately I knew I had said the wrong thing.

Her brows lowered. 'If I were you I'd have as little to do with Thady as possible. He spied on Brian and me and told Rowan of our plans. He's cunning and sly and, apart from his beloved pigs, I'd say he hates us and everything at Raheen cordially.' She planked a plate of greasy and burned food on the table and added grudgingly, 'All except Rowan, perhaps, and in his case it's not really liking; more a sort of respect: he feels Rowan is what they call in this part of the country, "a hard man". And how right he is!' she added bitterly.

As I tried to make a start on the unappetizing rashers I told myself that it was natural she should resent the presence of the servant who, she believed, had reported her movements to Rowan, but there was something exaggerated about her reaction and I began to wonder if, owing to her dislike for her brother, she was unconsciously dramatizing the situation.

She perched herself on the edge of the table and watched me morosely. 'I know I've made an awful mess of your breakfast,' she said contritely, 'and I'm sure the tea is much stronger than you like it. Now if you had had the luck to arrive after Emer marries Rowan you'd have found everything ship-shape. She's a terrific manager and Peggy tells me the Lacey servants are terrified of her temper.'

I placed my cup down and glanced across at her. Had there been a note of admiration in her voice when she spoke of Emer Lacey? Did she know of the extraordinary meeting between the girl and her brother on the previous night? I wondered, but her next words let me know she did.

'Did you hear the rumpus, last night?' she laughed. 'Emer is certainly completely uninhibited—but then that's the only type of girl Rowan would be interested in. She'll be a match for him when they marry: you see, Emer has always had her own way, ever since she was a little girl. Her mother died when she was a child and Mr Lacey dotes on her: in his eyes everything she does is perfect.'

'Is that altogether a good thing?' I asked quietly.

She glanced at me in faint irritation. 'I've always admired the way Emer grabs what she wants out of life. If I had had half her guts, things would have turned out differently for me.' She stared ahead in frowning silence for a moment, then said, 'I know you'll like Emer when you meet her. She has terrific style and poise, and I'd like you to be friends.'

Remembering the violence of her meeting with Rowan I had the feeling that Emer and I would hardly get along well together. However, Ita saved me thinking up some non-committal remark by crossing to the range, taking up the enormous brown earthenware teapot and filling up my cup with the thick dark brew. 'Emer was wonderful to me when she knew I was in love with Brian: she did everything in her power to help me get out of Rowan's clutches, for although she's crazy about him she understands how arbitrary and domineering he can be. When I told her I was going to run off with Brian she agreed it was the best line I could take. That's the type she is, truly loyal and sympathetic.'

Was this true? I wondered. Emer had not struck me as capable of putting herself out to assist another girl. On the other hand Ita herself was so sure that it was Thady who had given away her plans to Rowan! I found myself wondering guiltily why I should suspect Emer of treachery when I hadn't even met her.

It was at this point Bernie returned. 'There's a phone-call for you, Miss Ita,' she called from the door. 'It's Miss Emer and she says she wants to talk to you very particular.'

Ita's face brightened and to my relief she laid down the big teapot as she was on the point of topping up my cup. 'I shan't keep you a moment, Nicola,' she called as she hurried off.

Bernie surveyed me curiously for a moment. I could see she wasn't quite sure of my position at Raheen and was uncertain of what line to take with me. Slowly she collected a box of dusters and polishing materials from a cupboard and departed unenthusiastically.

When Ita returned her face was bright with happiness; all traces of sullenness had vanished and it struck me that this radiant girl was the Ita Brian Carbery had known and loved.

'Guess what! Emer has invited herself to dinner! She's terribly keen to meet you.' Ita gave a trill of amusement. 'She was quite open about it—but then that's Emer's way—there's no ladylike namby-pamby-ness as far as she's concerned.'

I found the idea of being looked over by Emer rather daunting. 'But—but why does she want to meet me?' I asked in dismay. 'I don't imagine I'm the type Emer would be even remotely interested in. I've been dancing attendance on people for years, while she's been cosseted and spoiled and given her own way: we'll be as different as chalk and cheese.'

Ita shrugged, then her eyes lit up with mischief. 'I shouldn't be at all surprised if she wants to see if you hold out any competition.'

'Competition?' I echoed blankly.

'Yes, everyone will be talking of the new English girl at Raheen and asking each other what's she like and if she's very grand; or friendly; or pretty; or dowdy: you've no idea what an interest we take in each other's lives in this part of the country. And of course Emer will be crazy to see if you're going to be dangerous as far as Rowan's concerned! It's typical of her to tackle it like this: she doesn't believe in being mealy-mouthed: she just goes for what she wants, bald-headed,' Ita said appreciatively.

'But it's utterly preposterous,' I said at last, feeling at a loss at such outrageous frankness. 'I don't even like your brother I resent his attitude: the assumption that I'm part of his goods and chattels. Why, the idea that I could be—be interested——' I choked with indignation.

'You forget,' Ita said dryly, 'Emer will be completely indifferent to your attitude towards Rowan. What will interest her will be how Rowan regards you.'

'Well, she needn't worry,' I said tartly. 'Rowan's attitude towards me will be only too plain: he sees me as a new part of the furnishings of Raheen, and when he does give me a thought it's to consider what a nuisance I'm going to be.'

Ita considered this judiciously as she collected the dishes. 'Perhaps! But at the same time you're pretty and I expect attractive to men. As to Rowan, I have no idea how he regards you—but then it's rather hard to know what he thinks.' she added tightly. 'Anyway, at present, I'm more concerned about what we're going to have for dinner tonight. It's just like Doreen to get laid up when Emer's coming to dinner. Doreen's a wonderful cook and, as you can see, I'm hopeless.' She pointed ruefully at the blackened pan.

'Perhaps I could help,' I said tentatively. 'Sometimes I helped with the cooking at The Hollies: at least, I could prepare simple dishes.'

Ita's eyes brightened. 'Oh, that would be wonderful! Emer's so good at everything. I'd feel such a fool dishing up one of my usual fiascos. What about a steak and salad and some sort of sweet? Can you think of something nice and unusual, Nicola?'

It was strange to see her usually brooding expression become gay with animation and enthusiasm.

I smiled. 'At The Hollies there was an old recipe book belonging to my aunt's grandmother. There was

80

one sweet in particular we were very fond of, especially at this time of the year when the autumn fruits are ready: it was called apple and blackberry soufflé: I don't know if it's particularly unusual, but it was a great favourite.'

'Then do make it,' Ita said eagerly. 'Later on you can collect what you need from the orchard and I'll supply the rest of the ingredients and have things ready for you.'

The morning passed quickly. Everything at Raheen was strange and unusual to me, and when Ita, as though showing a sign of her favour, took me on a tour of the Castle, I marvelled at its size and the thickness of some of the walls.

In the very oldest parts of the Castle the walls had had to be thick, Ita explained, because in days gone by this part of Ireland had been raided by the Danes. 'They say that's why we've so many redheads in this part of the world,' she laughed.

We were standing at the top of a tower leading off from a disused wing of the Castle and there was a view across the sea stretching to the limitless horizon. Not a sail was in sight and the craggy cliffs, pushing out into the water on each side of the cove, were dark and intimidating. 'A ship of the Spanish Armada was wrecked on Raheen Point.' Ita had to raise her voice against the salty wind that swept across the Castle. 'We have a goblet that's said to have been looted from the wreck by one of our ancestors and the story goes that he killed a man in the process. It shows what pretty shady characters the Delaneys could be.' She laughed as she turned and we retraced our steps down the stone corkscrew staircase. 'So beware, Nicola, that you don't fall into our clutches!'

She was joking, I knew, yet was it not true that something of his ruthless looting ancestors had been inherited by Rowan Delaney! Should they happen to be in accord at dinner, he and Emer would make a formidable pair, and I wished heartily that the evening were over.

I was convinced Emer Lacey would do everything in her power to make me feel uncomfortable and unwanted—not necessarily that she would consider me a rival, for no doubt, as far as she was concerned, I would appear beneath contempt, but rather that I felt sure she would view a newcomer as someone upon whom to sharpen her wits. There was certainly no point in questioning Ita, for it was obvious that as far as Ita was concerned her idol could do no wrong, and she, no doubt, would be amazed and perhaps amused if she guessed how I dreaded the coming evening.

Later we began to make preparations for the dinner, assisted by Peggy, who was a younger and plumper version of her cousin. In the orchard the crisp scents of autumn were in the air and among the grasses creamy-pink apples lay in drifts where they had been blown by the wind from the sea. I found the blackberries growing thickly on the side of a narrow boreen that wound up to the hillside fields and soon I had filled a can with the ripe juicy berries.

Strangely enough I had seen no flowers in any of the rooms of the Castle and, when I suggested I gather some for the long gloomy dining-room, Ita shrugged indifferently. 'Do if you like! Flower arrangement is not one of my ladylike accomplishments.'

She sounded contemptuous, and I wondered if this

was how she really felt or if it was rather the defence of someone acutely aware of her shortcomings when it came to home-making.

Drifts of blue and mauve michaelmas daisies grew at Raheen, the blooms much bigger than I remembered seeing them: here too the hydrangea had enormous blue and china-pink heads. I decided, however, to make a centre piece of the michaelmas daisies with sprays of the shiny orange bead-like fruit of the mountain ash and branches of waxen snow-berries that lined the avenue.

Bernie rummaged in one of the store-rooms and produced a heavy chunkily cut crystal vase. In it my arrangement looked vibrant and colourful against the dark red wood of the table.

Bernie clasped her hands together in admiration, then summoned Ita and Peggy to share her admiration.

Ita looked surprised. 'Well, I must say it looks terrific,' she said slowly. 'Did you learn to do that sort of thing, or does it come naturally, as the song says?'

Peggy and Bernie immediately collapsed into helpless laughter.

'Oh, cut it out, will you, girls,' Ita said crossly, and repeated her question.

'Neither really—although I've read a few books on the subject, but my aunt always liked me to do the flowers, as she had no gift for that sort of thing herself but loved to see them about the house.'

She sniffed. 'This is one house where you're not likely to see them—unless of course you do it yourself. In my opinion it's a complete waste of time and energy. After all, even if I stuffed Raheen with flowers,

I bet neither Rowan nor Derry would even notice—so what's the point?'

'You lie in your teeth,' a masculine voice said loudly from the door, and as they swung around to see the newcomer the two girls seized the opportunity to indulge in shrill screams of alarm.

'Oh, Mr Derry, you did frighten us so!' gasped Bernie.

'Yes, what with hearing Doreen say the Black Delaney rides around at night it's enough to make the hair stand up on your head,' Peggy announced triumphantly.

'Calm down, calm down!' Derry made soothing noises. 'No need to go into a tizzy—and for that matter, I bet you girls would be thrilled to bits if the Black Delaney happened to take the smallest notice of you.'

Amidst their giggling disclaimers Ita said, 'What are you doing here at this hour? Why aren't you at work?'

'You're beginning to sound like Rowan,' he said, without rancour. 'Well, for your information, I'm simply on my way to pick up a prospective customer, and it occurred to me that I might drop in for some light refreshment—and also to find out how Nicola is faring. After all,' he added grandly, 'she's by way of being a sort of relation of ours, aren't you, Cousin Nicola?'

His dark eyes were lazily insolent as they surveyed me.

'Rubbish!' Ita said caustically. 'And Nicola's not such a fool as to be taken in by your plamas. I expect it's simply an excuse to get out of work.'

He grinned, then said maliciously, 'You'll never be much of a success with the opposite sex, Ita, if you

84

persist in that blunt and forthright manner of yours. It's not the sort of thing to make a girl attractive.'

Ita laughed. It was obvious that, unlike her attitude towards Rowan, she regarded Derry with an elder sister's indulgence. 'It's time we were getting back to work,' she said, leading the way to the door. 'I don't want to be running around when Emer arrives.'

'So Emer's expected, is she?' Derry asked as we followed.

'Miss Emer rung up to say she was coming to dinner,' Bernie vouchsafed eagerly.

'And she always dressed lovely,' Peggy added rapturously. 'But then she's a real beauty, there's no denying that.'

'Huh!' Derry sounded non-committal, but I got the impression that he was not particularly pleased at the news.

He accompanied us to the kitchen and perched himself on the end of the table, swinging his legs and watching our activities with bright mischievous eyes. 'So Emer's coming to dinner?' he remarked when Peggy and Bernie had left the kitchen. 'Now I wonder what she's up to?'

Ita, who was passing the pulped fruits through a sieve, glanced at him irritably. 'You've always disliked Emer, haven't you, Derry? I wonder if it's because you've tried on the charm and found it didn't work with her?'

Derry rolled his eyes ceilingwards in mock disclaimer. 'Perish the thought! So help me, I've never as much as raised my eyes to the fair creature. In her imperious presence I am struck dumb with admiration. Should she but deign to cast the bright radiance

85

of her glance in my direction I am transported with delight.'

Ita snorted. 'Drivel! You can't stand Emer, and never could.'

Coolly Derry leaned forward, scooped up a portion of the white of egg which I had beaten into a froth and popped it into his mouth. 'Well, now that you come to mention it, I admit I can't stand the girl.'

'Ha,' Ita crowed triumphantly, 'and I bet I'm right. She probably put you firmly in your place when you began that Casanova routine you give every girl who crosses your path.'

I remembered my first meeting with Derry and his assumption that I would instantly succumb to his charms and wondered if she were right concerning her brother.

'I know you don't credit me with any discrimination when it comes to an attractive woman, but it happens that you're wrong,' he replied flatly. 'Fact is, I don't necessarily fall for a girl just because she happens to be ravishingly beautiful like Emer Lacey.'

His words were calm and measured, and Ita glanced at him doubtfully. 'Well, why do you dislike her so much?'

Derry licked the last particle of egg white from his finger. 'Because I think she's a treacherous, double-dealing little hellcat, and if you'd a grain of sense you'd have seen through her ages ago. She's out to get Rowan and simply uses you as a means to an end.'

Ita's face grew pale with rage and shock and I saw her fingers grow tight about the bowl of puree. Then, before I realized what she had in mind, she raised it shoulder high and was on the point of hurling its contents over her grinning brother when I sprang to life.

'Don't, Ita!' I shouted, leaning across the table and grasping the bowl.

Slowly Ita lowered it to the table. 'Sorry, Nicola,' she said contritely. 'It was rotten of me—especially when you've been such a help. Anyway,' she added, glancing at an old-fashioned wag-o'-the-wall, 'we wouldn't have had time to make more!'

There was a short pause after this astounding remark, then suddenly, to my amazement, both Derry and his sister dissolved into helpless screams of laughter. I joined in, but without any real amusement, my heart still beating nervously at Ita's barely averted violence. How many shocks and alarms would I have to endure, I wondered ruefully, before I became inured to the Delaneys' wild mercurial temperament?

It was only when our preparations were complete and I had gone up to my room and opened my wardrobe that I realized I had nothing suitable to wear. My shabby faded beige wool dress had not been improved by dark blackberry stains and all Joyce's other offerings, with the exception of the negligée, had the seedy limp look of articles of clothing in a jumble sale. I could hardly appear in my apricot negligée, however, I thought gloomily, then wondered why I wanted so passionately to look my best. After all, until then I had worn Joyce's cast-offs without complaint! Was it because I knew Emer would be perfectly groomed and exquisitely gowned that I loathed appearing in front of her as the poor relation?

I was still standing in front of the wardrobe, glumly surveying its contents, when Ita came in. Her hair was smoothed back into a tight coil and a simple dress of bark-brown with a wide Puritan collar gave her calm oval face a grave ethereal look. 'Not ready yet, Nicola?' She seemed surprised.

I shook my head. 'I shan't be long,' I said in confusion.

But she crossed to the wardrobe and standing beside me surveyed its contents with frowning interest. 'But surely these colours are not right for you?'

This was so true that, surprised, I found myself stammering that they had belonged to Joyce.

'Poor Nicola,' she said, when I had finished, 'what a horrid cousin she must have been to have wished such rubbish on you.'

Again the Delaney candour embarrassed me and as I began some halting excuse she interrupted peremptorily, 'You must let me lend you a frock. I don't know if you'll like any of my things, but at least they won't be so depressing and shabby.' With a little gesture of finality she shut the wardrobe door and led the way to her room.

I was a little surprised to see how extensive Ita's wardrobe was somehow I had gathered from her forthright, almost boyish manner, that she would not be particularly interested in clothes.

She seemed to guess my thoughts as we riffled through the racks of dresses and coats that had all the appearance of never having been worn. 'I got these after I met Brian,' she said hesitantly. 'I wanted so much to appear to advantage. I suppose I thought they would make up for my other deficiencies.' She shrugged and smiled bitterly, then added brusquely, 'Well, do you see anything you might like?'

Hastily I selected a simply cut frock of honey-coloured crushed velvet, banded at throat and sleeves and around the straight skirt-line with the same material in lime green. As I slipped into it I realized that my choice had been lucky: it suited me perfectly, the honey tones highlighting my hair and reflecting on my skin, giving it a golden glow.

When we went downstairs Rowan had returned. He was mixing drinks at the cabinet when we entered the hall and raised his eyebrows as he regarded us quizzically. 'What are all the fine feathers for? And what in heaven's name have you done with Nicola? She looks very grand: no longer the little orphan of the storm.'

'I gave her one of my frocks,' Ita said complacently. For once her enmity towards her brother seemed to be forgotten. 'She had nothing but some beastly hand-me-downs.' She regarded me with a proprietorial air. 'Yes, it certainly makes a difference.'

I felt my temper rise to boiling point. How typical of the Delaneys to discuss me as if I were inanimate and my feelings and reactions of no importance!

'Here,' Rowan said coolly, pushing a glass into my unwilling hand, 'take this and relax. You look as if you intended to explode. But don't! For I can assure you that at Raheen we're inured to displays of violence and temperament.'

'All except Emer's temperaments,' Ita put in. 'She can be quite devastating when she wants to.' She crossed to the window. 'She should be here any minute: she has one of those low fast cars and cuts a terrific dash about the countryside.' Again I noticed her tones of admiration and I guessed that she herself longed to have the panache of her friend.

'What's this about Emer?' Rowan asked sharply.

'Simply that she invited herself to dinner,' Ita replied happily.

'I see! So that accounts for the fine feathers!' His voice was dry and I wished for a moment I had kept on my old beige woollen dress. I had the feeling he guessed that I had dressed to hold my own with the glamorous Emer. I wished so much to appear cool and detached, yet the fact that I had gone to the trouble of borrowing a dress for the occasion seemed to give her visit an importance I was loath to admit.

'Here she is,' Ita announced from her post at the window.

CHAPTER SIX

FAINTLY, then nearer and nearer, came the roar of a powerful car as it tore along the avenue.

Derry, who had entered the room and was helping himself to a drink from a cabinet, grinned mischievously. 'One of these days Emer will break that beautiful neck of hers. Why don't you marry the girl, Rowan, and put her out of her misery?'

I saw Rowan stiffen: his hard-featured face darkened as he turned towards his brother.

Before he could speak, Ita said anxiously, 'Oh, for heaven's sake, Derry, why must you start a brawl just when we're expecting a guest?'

Derry shrugged. 'I can't see why my simple words should cause a furore. After all, Emer herself has never hidden the fact that she's crazy to marry him.'

I felt my throat tighten at Derry's outrageously obvious effort to needle his brother, then to my relief, there was the sound of quick light footsteps and Emer Lacey appeared in the doorway.

For a moment she stood there poised, a lithe elegant figure in a dress slashed in bold crimson and turquoise. Her red hair was caught up with a velvet ribbon in a wild tangle of ringlets that fell in gypsy abandon to her white shoulders. Her apricot lips parted, showing small even teeth. Slanted sea-green eyes crinkled into a smile. 'I thought I'd catch you all here,' she said, her voice high and light, with a strangely attractive little catch in some of the words. She advanced into the room, perfectly at her ease, as though unaware of the effect she created by her exotic beauty.

As Ita introduced me, Emer gave me a glance of candid appraisal, her eyes almost childlike in her eager innocence.

I felt completely at a loss. Remembering the scene outside my window on the previous night, I had been expecting a termagant, and yet this beautiful gracious girl with the appealing look in her green eyes seemed to offer me nothing but friendship.

Her fiery curls flared on her shoulders as she turned towards Rowan. 'It's fairly obvious why you developed strong family feelings, Rowan,' she said with a little tinkle of laughter.

'I'm afraid I don't quite follow,' he replied dryly.

Emer made a moue. 'Don't pretend to be obtuse. When a girl is as pretty as Nicola, a man would be a fool not to make the most of a so-called relationship.'

'You're wrong, Emer,' Rowan said as he mixed her a drink. 'I had no idea what Nicola's appearance would be when I called on her.' He paused and looked across at me derisively as he handed her a glass. 'For all I knew she might have been as ugly as sin.'

To my annoyance I felt myself colour with embarrassment.

Emer sipped her drink and regarded him over the brim. 'How noble of you, Rowan darling! So you intended to claim the relationship even if Nicola had proved to be a dreadful old frump? What a strong family feeling you must have,' she said ingenuously.

'He'll make some lucky woman a wonderful husband, won't he, Emer?' Derry put in maliciously.

For a moment the green eyes lost their softness and

glittered with the coldness of an emerald.

To everyone's relief, at that moment Peggy popped her head in and after eyeing Emer's dress and hairstyle with open approval, said, 'Bernie and myself will dish up, just as soon as the company's ready, Miss Ita.' When Ita nodded her consent, she withdrew her head and shut the door with a loud thud.

Emer gave her strange attractive bubbling little laugh. 'I do envy you the girls, Ita, they're so quaint and amusing.'

I could see, however, that her casual words had upset Ita. 'I'm afraid they're altogether too slapdash,' she said worriedly, 'but then I'm not really a good housekeeper and the girls have found that out long ago.'

As we entered the dining-room I felt a little glow of satisfaction at the attractive appearance of the table, now lit with crimson candles, but as the meal commenced I could see that Ita was irritably aware of Peggy's and Bernie's shortcomings and, much to their affronted surprise, she occasionally spoke to them sharply for chatting animatedly as they served. Was there a look of satisfaction in Emer's green eyes as she witnessed her friend's discomfiture? I wondered, then dismissed the idea, for as the meal progressed, Emer's charm scintillated like a sharply cut diamond. Even Derry, I could see, in spite of his distrust and animosity, was succumbing to her blandishments.

Gradually my memories of the previous night—the upraised arm which had struck so viciously at Rowan —assumed the vague nebulous outlines of a dream. It was impossible to imagine this gay, charming girl as a wild virago.

My thoughts were brought back to the present by hearing her say interestedly, 'Now who arranged those flowers so beautifully? I know it wasn't you, Ita, for you despise such feminine activities.'

Ita smiled good-naturedly. 'Actually it was Nicola. I agree, she has done it beautifully.'

'Mountain ash, snowberries and michaelmas daisies —how unusual!' Emer said musingly. 'And now I wonder if it was an association of ideas, as the psychologists put it.'

'I can't say I follow you,' Derry remarked, his eyes bright and watchful.

'Simply that mountain ash is also known as rowan, isn't it?' She glanced across at me with an air of eager interest. 'It's probably only a coincidence, but if I were Rowan I'd be flattered.'

I gazed back at her in confusion, not quite sure how to receive this remark.

It was Rowan, however, who riveted her attention. 'Nicola is a well-brought-up young lady who doesn't believe in pandering to a man's vanity. I very much doubt if she had me in mind when she made her charming arrangement, so if I were you I wouldn't pursue that line of country, Emer.' He sounded brusque and there was a moment's silence when I saw the green eyes narrow and flicker with rage at this cavalier treatment and I got the impression that it was only a mighty effort of will-power that she controlled the urge to answer him in kind.

Ita looked from one to the other anxiously and I felt a growing sympathy and pity for the girl: it was so obvious she wanted the dinner to be a success, yet experience had taught her that Emer's moods were unpredictable.

It was Derry who, strangely enough, managed to steer the conversation into safer channels. He made appreciative noises as Peggy entered, bearing the sweet. 'Now why haven't we had something like this before?' he asked, as he demolished a large helping.

'Because Nicola arrived only yesterday,' his sister replied with a smile.

'From now on I can expect some delicious and exotic confection daily from your dainty hands,' Derry said decisively.

'I'm afraid not,' I said ruefully. 'That's about my only accomplishment. My services weren't called on at The Hollies except in emergencies, so I haven't really had a lot of experience.'

Emer raised her brows enquiringly as though waiting for me to enlarge on my past history and when I closed my mouth firmly, determined not to be questioned by her, much to my discomfiture, Ita, as though anxious to placate her friend, said eagerly, 'Oh, Nicola was staying with her aunt and cousin. It was splendid that Rowan insisted on bringing her back to Raheen, for they were obviously making a little slave of her.'

'Slave!' Emer repeated with a laugh. 'Well, I must say she doesn't give that impression.' Her eyes ran over my frock with expert appraisal. 'Quite an expensive get-up for a slave-girl!'

'Oh, but poor Nicola had only the most awful hand-me-downs when she came to Raheen. Hadn't you, Nicola?' Ita rushed on. 'Actually I lent her that frock.' She paused as though aware that she might have given offence and glanced across at me. 'You don't mind my saying that, do you, Nicola?'

I shook my head, speechless with mortification. It was obvious that Ita already considered Emer as one of the family and had an almost childish faith in her friendship. But it was a confidence I couldn't share. There was something much too cold and calculating about the slanted green eyes for me to adopt Ita's attitude of complete trust.

Gradually, as the conversation turned to local characters and events of which I knew nothing, I let my mind drift. It was pleasant in the long-shadowed room, the crimson candles glittering on the silver and crystal and casting reflections on the dark-old-fashioned furniture and faded gilt of the portraits.

'I believe old Daisy Tarrant is auctioning off part of the collection,' I heard Emer remark idly.

Immediately a little ripple of laughter passed around the table and Derry turned to me, his eyes gleaming with merriment. 'Mrs Tarrant is by way of being one of our local characters. You'll understand why when you meet her. Her husband was an extremely astute judge of antiques and she has inherited a unique collection of eighteenth-century knick-knacks.'

'Will you be going, Rowan?' Emer asked.

'Now why on earth should I attend the auction?' Rowan asked with an air of amusement. 'Do you see me as the type that collects snuff-boxes and quizzing-glasses?'

Emer shrugged. 'Perhaps not, but I should have thought you'd have been keen to keep the Black De-laney's ring in the family.'

Rowan frowned. 'You mean she's selling that too? I should have thought she'd have given us the chance to buy it back.'

Emer laughed gleefully. 'Not Daisy Tarrant! It seems she has informed the entire countryside that if you want your devil of an ancestor's ring, you can go to Galway and bid for it.'

'I see,' Rowan's lips tightened. 'Then let the wretched thing go to the highest bidder!'

'Oh, Rowan, let's keep the ring in the family,' Ita said impulsively.

I guessed it was a long time since she had addressed him with such an air of eagerness and lack of bitterness and I saw him glance up with an expression of pleased surprise. 'I mean,' she went on hurriedly, 'it really should belong to us—it's—a sort of heirloom.'

'And just how do you come to that conclusion?' he asked with a gentleness I had never heard in his voice before.

'Well, you know the story——' She hesitated and paled.

In the intense silence that followed Emer turned to me and said in her high attractive voice, 'It's really quite a romantic story. The Black Delaney fell madly in love with one of the beautiful Tarrant sisters whom he met at the court of the Regent. He gave her his ring and they planned to elope. However, her father got wind of their plans and brought her back to Ireland. Soon afterwards she died of a broken heart, but, in spite of the Black Delaney's notorious reputation, the Tarrants kept the jewel in their family.'

I guessed it was the memory of her own plans to elope that had upset Ita. However, Emer seemed sublimely unaware of any uncomfortable undercurrents. 'Ita's right, you must definitely secure it, Rowan.

After all, it's the betrothal ring of the Delaneys.' Her voice rang out hard and insistent and I saw Rowan's face soften at the vibrant beauty of her flushed cheeks and sea-green eyes.

'Your wish is my command,' he said, his voice lowered, as though shutting out the rest of us and isolating them in a world of their own. 'Ita will bid for it when the time comes.'

He glanced across at his sister, who nodded grudgingly as though regretting her earlier civility.

'I was looking forward to our making a day of it,' Emer said sharply.

'Sorry, it's quite impossible. We're much too busy for me to be able to take a day off, even for the Delaney ring. However it should make a break for Nicola: the Tarrant collection is supposed to be outstanding and Daisy herself is quite unique in her own way: she'll undoubtedly attend the auction.'

'Showing Nicola our local eccentrics is not my idea of an amusing day,' Emer said tightly. The light from the windows had faded and her eyes glittered angrily in the candlelight.

Ita glanced anxiously at her friend, obviously recognizing the storm signals.

'And to think there's hardly a man in the length and breadth of the country who wouldn't jump at the chance of spending a day with you! If I were you I wouldn't put up with such treatment,' Derry said with mock solicitude. His face seemed hollow and shadowed and he looked like a malignant satyr in the flickering light.

Emer's eyes narrowed ominously. 'Derry's right.' She had raised her voice. All pretence of gentle femininity had disappeared: there was something elemental and primitive about her manner and I realized my hands were clasped together nervously. 'If the ring and all it stands for mean so little to you, then I shan't go at all,' she gritted.

Rowan gazed across at her impassively and I understood something of the frustration that drove her to such lengths. With all other men her smallest desire would be met with instant acquiescence, but with Rowan Delaney she was dealing with a character strong and resilient as steel, yet the very novelty of confronting someone able to withstand her dangerous beauty must in itself be a challenge. That Rowan Delaney had chinks in his armour she already knew only too well. The memory of that moment in the moonlight when he had taken her in his arms must have been like sweet heady wine. To admit defeat now in front of us would be intolerable.

Ita glanced across at me appealingly, evidently hoping I would be able to interpose some bright and interesting remark that would divert the protagonists.

Peggy had entered the room now and was dawdling at the sideboard eagerly stacking dishes, evidently loath to miss a single word: stowing away all details to be recounted later in the kitchen to her cousin and Thady.

'Look, let's settle this matter amicably,' Derry said with an air of sweet reasonableness. 'I'll take you. As a member of the Delaney clan my presence will ensure that your honour is vindicated and you can wear the wretched thing back to Raheen. Can't she, Rowan?'

There was no doubting his intentions. He was deliberately goading both Emer and his brother and I dreaded the scene that I knew was bound to ensue.

'Keep out of this,' Rowan grated, his eyes still fixed on Emer's angry face.

Derry shrugged with an air of mock resignation. 'Oh, very well! Just trying to keep the path of true love running smooth!'

'Are you or are you not going to take me to Galway?' Emer stormed.

'I've already told you I can't,' Rowan said quietly. 'You seem to be under the impression that I can drop work whenever it suits your whim.'

Emer sprang to her feet. In the suddenness and violence of her movement her shoe caught in the edge of the lace tablecloth, jerking it forward. With a crash the crystal vase in the centre of the table overturned: water spilled across the cloth and dripped slowly to the floor and the table was spattered with white and orange berries.

Completely indifferent to the havoc she had wrought, Emer turned, brushing past Peggy, who had been watching with wide-eyed amazement, and the candles flickered wildly as she crashed the door behind her.

There was a long pause after her departure during which Peggy, all agog, slipped from the room. Rowan's strong brown fingers played with the stem of his glass. Then I heard what he had been waiting for, the sound of a car driven furiously down the avenue.

Ita got to her feet, her face pale, like a cameo cut out of white jade. 'Why didn't you agree to take her, Rowan? After all, you could have found the time if you had wanted to. I sometimes think you deliberately thwart Emer just to prove something to yourself.'

'No, you're wrong there, Ita. It's to prove something to Emer—that not all men are her toys and playthings.'

Ita's manner was composed, but not even the soft flattery of candlelight could disguise the livid scar that marred the pale beauty of her skin. A faint derisive smile touched her lips. 'Yet you've every intention of marrying her one fine day.'

'That remains to be seen,' he replied evenly.

She shook her head as she moved towards the door, then said bitterly, 'Emer's not like me: she's one of those girls who are on the winning side—and what's more I admire her for it.'

'Well, every man to his own poison,' Derry said cheerfully, as he followed his sister. 'Personally I'd rather a nice homely type who'd be waiting for me with hot slippers and a list of her domestic woes.'

But that was exactly what a man like Rowan didn't want in his wife, I realized with a little twinge. There was something too deep and turbulent in his own nature to be satisfied with the type of girl Derry had so aptly described.

When we were alone he sat back in his chair gazing frowningly ahead as though unaware that I was in the room with him.

Then suddenly the tension that had been building up before Emer's stormy departure overwhelmed me and, to hide the nervous tremor of my hands, I picked up the overturned vase and rather ineffectually began to mop at the water with my napkin and gather up the scattered branches that were strewn across the tablecloth.

As I straightened I became aware that Rowan was

now standing directly behind me, and as I turned with my arms full of the colourful foliage he put his hands on my shoulders and looked gravely into my eyes. 'Surely you haven't let Emer's dramatics upset you, Nicola?' He sounded impatient, as though intolerant of such weakness.

I gazed back at him resentfully. 'Obviously you haven't let her dramatics upset you!'

'No. It's simply that a beauty like Emer is so used to getting her own way that it infuriates her to be baulked. I've found less beautiful women, too, have their methods of getting their own way.'

In spite of the faint contempt in his voice I couldn't resist saying, 'Such as?'

He looked amused. 'Perhaps they adopt the method Derry described: slippers by the fireside, the ties of domestic life.'

'And of course that's the sort of life you despise!'

For a moment he looked thoughtful. 'Strange as it may sound, I've never really met a woman with such accomplishments.'

'If you had?' I insisted.

His strong blunt fingers outlined the curve of my eyebrow, then traced, almost absently, across my cheekbones. 'You're very pretty,' he said thoughtfully, 'and very persistent. Is it because you hate me so much and long to prove to yourself what a disagreeable person I am?'

I drew back as though his words had stung, for I realized that, in spite of my resolution not to allow myself to be domineered by him, my intense interest in the man was subtly placing me in his power.

His hands dropped to his sides. 'So you don't intend

to co-operate, is that it? No doubt you still wish yourself back at The Hollies, dancing attendance on your cousin, or listening to the inanities of that foolish aunt of yours? If so,' he added harshly, 'you're a fool.'

Perhaps, I thought bitterly, but at least at The Hollies I could preserve a certain amount of detachment. Here at Raheen I was hurled into the fierce antagonisms and cross-currents of the Delaneys, and worst of all was the knowledge that I could not be indifferent to Rowan Delaney. My very dislike of him was a sort of bondage and now I hit back, all the burning resentment I felt towards him spilling out in my words.

'How dare you speak of my aunt and cousin as though they were some sort of inferior species! You forget they didn't mean to be unkind. According to their lights they considered they'd done pretty well by me: they took me in when I had nowhere else to go, just as you took me in when I had the prospect of being left without a home. Do you imagine that, here at Raheen, I'm happier than I was at The Hollies? What chance have I of keeping Ita's friendship if she finds out that I'm supposed to earn my keep by acting a sort of glorified watchdog?'

He frowned. 'So that's how you see yourself?'

'What other way could I?'

'Isn't it possible you could visualize yourself taking your place as part of the family?'

'With you as the boss?' I returned swiftly.

'Why not? Whether you like it or not the fact remains that I am head of the Delaney family and fully intend to shoulder my responsibilities.'

'And you expect me to fit into the background, taking my place and doing as I'm told—as befits a destitute relation? Isn't that it?' I demanded.

'What exactly do you want, Nicola?' he asked frowningly.

Words rushed to my tongue, searing and self-revealing; words that would have told him I longed to be more to him than a tiresome responsibility, forced to sit quietly and self-effacingly at his table while I watched the admiration in his dark eyes as Emer, her copper hair glowing in the candlelight, faced him like a furious and beautiful tigress. But I struggled for control before the fatal irrevocably humiliating admission could be made.

'The girls will want to clear up,' I said dully, and turned away from him.

But before I could go, he came close to me and kissed me lightly on the forehead. 'Poor Nicola, you make life so very difficult and complicated for yourself! I'm beginning to get the idea that I've a stormy petrel on my hands.'

How different this cool impersonal kiss was from the embrace that I had witnessed in the moonlight! Dismayed at the surge of turbulent feeling that left me helpless, I stood still as a statue, in case a sudden involuntary movement should reveal the longing I felt to be held close in his arms.

CHAPTER SEVEN

As the days passed I began to settle in to the easy-going, unconventional life at Raheen. The weather was mild although around us the foliage and flowers showed signs that autumn had set in in earnest. The hydrangeas kept their perfect shape, the once pastel pink and blue blossoms turned to dull umber. On the hills too the bracken was rusty brown and in the still warm air the foliage that remained on the trees hung loosely from the branches like gold and copper medallions, yet the shortness of the days made me realize that winter could not be long delayed. My stay at Raheen was to be merely a temporary measure, I told myself, and I longed to grasp the beauty of these heavenly days.

Doreen, a stout pleasant-faced woman, returned to her duties and both Bernie and Peggy, I noticed, had much more respect for her wishes than they had for Ita's, for, in spite of her evident good-nature, Doreen ruled the kitchen with a rod of iron and Thady's mild flirtations with the girls came to an abrupt halt. It was Doreen herself now who brought me early morning tea, every bit as strong as Ita's brew but accompanied by slices of fresh wheaten bread and newly churned butter.

Some weeks later an incident occurred which taught me just how possessive Emer was as far as Rowan was concerned.

I awoke to find Doreen pulling the curtains, flooding the room with clear autumn light. 'Miss Ita's set on a picnic down in the cove,' she announced as she placed my morning tray on the bedside table and watched with satisfaction as I sipped sleepy-eyed at the dark bitter tea. 'And sure why shouldn't she, for these pet days won't last, you may be sure, and besides, she's mad keen on the swimming—not that she's as good as Mr Rowan, though it's not often he has the time for it.'

As she chattered on she moved about the room straightening ornaments and draperies, and I was on the point of asking her if Rowan was to accompany us, then bit back the words, fearful that her twinkling eye would read more into the query than I intended.

'There's no work today at the mines,' she continued, 'so no doubt Mr Rowan will go with you, though I wouldn't say the same for Mr Derry, for he's a great one for heading for the city any time he has the opportunity.'

When she had gone I got up reluctantly. I was not looking forward to the outing. Both Ita and Rowan were good swimmers and I knew that I would show up to disadvantage—something I wanted to avoid as much as possible where Rowan was concerned.

Apart from that, although an uneasy truce existed between brother and sister, I dreaded the scene that might ensue should Rowan catch sight of Brian Carbery perched on the rocks gazing out to sea as he kept his solitary vigil.

As we went through the wicket gate in the orchard the wind caught Ita's long dark hair, blowing it back from her face: a faint pinkness tinged her pale skin and she was chatting animatedly, and I saw Rowan, who was carrying a wicker picnic hamper, glance at his sister with pleased satisfaction.

To my relief, when we reached the cliff path I could see the cove was deserted. There was no sign of Brian's thin scholarly figure, only gulls swooping and diving against the clear translucent sky and scattered white clouds.

Ita was the first to enter the sea. She dived from a tall column of rock that jutted into the deep waters, then swam swiftly towards the horizon. Rowan and I watched as her bright blue cap receded further and further from the shore. 'Don't you think she's gone out far enough?' I asked anxiously.

Rowan, who was sprawled on a rug, gazed up at me mockingly. 'Don't worry, she swims like a fish. I shouldn't have thought you were the nervous type, Nicola.'

I gazed down at the sand I was riffling through my fingers and said defensively, 'She's so frightfully intense about everything she does—but then that's the Delaney character, isn't it?'

'And you don't approve of it?'

'Well, it does make life so complicated and involved.'

He clasped his hands behind his head and squinted up at the bright sky. 'So you still haven't come to terms with the Delaney temperament! How disappointing, especially as you'll have to live with it!'

His calm assumption that I had no other choice infuriated me. 'That's just where you're wrong!'

'And what exactly do you intend to do? I should be interested to hear your plans.'

He was openly mocking me, I realized with a feeling of helplessness. Derry had told me how closely knit the local community was and I had no doubt that his wishes would carry weight with our neighbours should I try to look for employment in the district. All he had to do was drop a hint to any family I approached that he did not wish them to employ me in any capacity and I should be forced to stay on at Raheen.

'Are we really so very dreadful, Nicola?'

I turned my head as I felt his eyes fixed on me. How incredibly mortifying if he should guess that I feared the hold he was securing over my heart and that I longed to escape before I had forged my own bonds; unable to part from him, yet without the hope of ever having his love. The prospect was terrifying to contemplate.

I gazed out to sea, my eyes blinded with tears, and he reached up his finger and gently brushed my face. 'You're crying,' he said wonderingly.

I was on the point of getting to my feet with a sudden impulsive gesture, but a glance at his face told me that all the derision had left his eyes and his lean-jawed face looked as hard as the dark rocks around.

'What's wrong, Nicola?' His hand shot out and clasped my wrist so that the sand spilled out of my fingers in a sudden gush.

I shook my head and said inanely, 'Thank goodness I see Ita turning back.'

'Never mind Ita,' he said roughly. His fingers tightened about my wrist. 'You haven't answered my question.'

'And I don't intend to,' I said wildly. 'Do leave go of my wrist.' I glanced up at the cliff, where a car had drawn up, aware that we presented an interesting spectacle to its occupant.

'Never mind the damn car!' he said angrily.

But at that moment there was the sound of the car door crashing to and Emer came scrambling down the cliff path towards us. 'They told me at the house that you'd gone swimming, so I borrowed this.' She gaily waved a cherry-red bathing suit. 'I shan't be a moment changing, then I'll race you out to the wreck, Rowan.' Without waiting for his reply she ran towards the cave, as Ita reached us, pulling the bathing-cap from her hair.

'I see Emer has arrived.' She looked pleased and exhilarated by her swim. 'I do hope Doreen has packed enough food for us all.'

'By the weight of the hamper I'd say she's stocked enough for a regiment,' Rowan said dryly.

Ita nodded happily. 'I'm glad, for Emer has what's called "a healthy appetite". It beats me how she keeps so wonderfully slim. I must ask her what the secret is.'

'What secret?' Emer asked as she rejoined us. She stood poised against the background of dark rock, her skin smooth as alabaster, her bronze-red hair cascading on to her shoulders.

In spite of myself I couldn't help glancing covertly across at Rowan to see his reaction to the tableau she presented. He looked darkly inscrutable, as though deliberately intent on withholding all signs of emotion.

Ita laughed and said brightly, 'I was saying I wonder how you keep so wonderfully slim.'

'Three sweet thoughts every morning,' Emer said lightly.

'I find that hard to believe.' Rowan's voice was dry. She tilted her head at him and made a moue. 'Now you're being horrid! Come on, I'll race you to the wreck.'

He shook his head. 'Not today. I'll leave that to Ita and yourself. After all, it's seldom I get a chance to rest my weary bones.'

'Yes, let's go.' Ita pulled on her bathing-cap again. 'The water's wonderful today, just right for seeing the wreck. Nicola can keep Rowan company.'

But Emer hesitated, scuffing at the sand with her pink lacquered toes. 'And why shouldn't Nicola come as well?' Her green eyes fixed me challengingly. 'You can swim, can't you? According to the gossip at Drumbeg you're a bit of a fanatic and take a dip nearly every morning.'

Before I could reply, Rowan put in swiftly, 'She's not by any means fanatical about swimming: in fact, she's not really very good.'

I turned on him indignantly. 'What do you mean? I can swim fairly well.'

'Exactly, "fairly well". I've often watched you from the cliff, so I have a pretty good idea of your ability. It takes more than fairly good swimming to reach the wreck, the currents are too dangerous.'

'Oh, not if you know your way about. Ita and I will take good care of her, won't we, Ita?'

Ita nodded, adopting something of her friend's contemptuous tone. 'Yes, we'll see she's perfectly safe.'

'Nevertheless, I don't think she should go,' Rowan said shortly. 'A weak swimmer can be swept away very swiftly. It is much too dangerous for Nicola.'

'Oh, don't be so ridiculously solicitous, Rowan.' Emer said with a spurt of anger. 'I've told you we'll take good care of your precious little treasure.'

I stood there feeling helpless and confused as they wrangled. Then Ita, who had gone to the water's edge and was waiting impatiently, called out, 'Well, are you coming, Nicola?'

I knew that the hulk of an old galleon wrecked on Raheen Point about three hundred years previously could be glimpsed on days when the water was especially clear, and I was anxious not to miss what would probably be the last opportunity to see it before the storms of autumn arrived. Besides, I was nettled by Emer's contemptuous attitude and even more by Rowen's attempts to dissuade me. 'You needn't bother arguing about it,' I announced firmly. 'I've decided to go, but don't put yourself out for me, Emer, for in spite of what Rowan says, I'm pretty well able to take care of myself.'

At my words I saw a forbidding frown gather on Rowan's craggy brow, but before he could intervene, I flung off the towelling wrap I had worn, raced down to the water's edge and plunged in after Ita.

'Follow me!' she called, and I struck out after her bobbing blue cap.

The water was cold but exhilarating and I felt excited and adventurous. I had not ventured near Raheen Point since Ita had warned me of the dangerous currents and I had the feeling that she herself would not have agreed to my going if it had not been for Emer's insistence and the underlying suggestion that Rowan was being unnecessarily cautious.

In spite of my efforts to make up with Ita, it wasn't long before I fell back and Emer passed me out, calling something over her shoulder that could have been a taunt or a warning or an encouragement. My arms felt like leaden weights as I battled on. Then suddenly I was filled with panic as I felt an undertow pull at my legs: Emer had forged so far ahead I realized that even if I called to her it was unlikely she would be able to hear me.

Then suddenly I caught sight of Ita: her arm was raised and she was waving to me, but whether in encouragement or warning I was too far away to tell. I drew a deep breath and struck off towards her and immediately I was seized by a strong current that swept me away as helpless as a piece of driftwood. For an instant I caught a glimpse of Ita's blue cap: was it imagination or was it now much nearer? Hope gave way to despair as I realized my own weakness and knew that long before she could reach me I should have been pulled beneath the glassy waves, floating lifeless to join those who had drowned there, hundreds of years ago in those treacherous currents.

I gave a scream of terror and struggled wildly before the current sucked me down and the waters closed over my head, and I was only vaguely conscious that two strong arms had grasped me firmly. With a sort of numb wonder I once more saw the sky above me and a voice was shouting something in my ear that I was unable to grasp.

Afterwards I had no recollection of how I had been brought ashore until I found myself being carried limply across the sands in Rowan's arms. 'Well, are you satisfied with yourself?' he demanded harshly, before dumping me none too gently on to the rug and tossing towards me my wrap.

He crossed to the picnic hamper and poured out a cup of hot coffee and was holding it to my lips when

Ita and Emer raced across the shingle towards us. Both, I noticed, looked white and shocked.

Emer was the first to recover. She gave a slightly nervous laugh. 'Really, if I'd known what a rotten swimmer you are I shouldn't have suggested the idea in the first place.'

'Wouldn't you?' Rowan swung towards her savagely and she started back at the anger that blazed in his dark eyes. 'Why did you encourage her when I told you she's a poor swimmer?'

'Because she wanted to go herself. She should have had enough sense to know she wasn't able for it.'

'It's fairly obvious she hasn't,' he said acidly, 'otherwise I shouldn't have had to do a rescuing act.' He sounded disgruntled as he rubbed his hair dry with a towel.

I sat up and said, with cold dignity, 'I'm sorry I put you to the trouble.'

He grinned suddenly. 'Think nothing of it! And now I suggest you go into the cave and change. We can have something to eat when you're ready.'

Ita nodded with a relieved air. 'Yes, let Emer and yourself change first and I'll set the things out and have a meal ready when you come back.'

In the cave we changed in silence. Emer seemed pre-occupied and I had the uneasy feeling that she was turning over in her mind some scheme.

When we returned Ita had unpacked the picnic basket and spread out, on a prettily printed cloth under the lee of a rock, chicken salad, slices of Doreen's crusty yeast bread that she religiously cooked each Friday and some of her delicious tarts, made from the last of the late peaches: coffee and a tall cool-looking bottle of white wine completed the meal.

'Yum, that does look good,' Emer said gaily, as she slumped down beside Rowan. 'I do envy you having Doreen; she's such a wonderful cook.'

Ita nodded as she poured coffee from a thermos jug. 'Yes, but it's a pity she's so superstitious—and she gets plenty of encouragement in this part of the country. The latest story is that she's seen the Black Delaney romping up and down the avenue and she insists on Thady escorting her back to the lodge every evening.'

'Probably looking for notice!' Rowan said, as he gnawed at a drumstick. 'A useful ploy to keep Thady on the straight-and-narrow.'

'A typical male reaction!' Emer jibed. 'But wouldn't it be romantic if it were true, and the Black Delaney were really haunting the Castle? How I'd love to meet him, looking fabulously handsome in those tricorn hats they used to wear and lots of gorgeous lace.'

'He'll probably be wearing a mask and carrying a pistol,' Rowan put in dryly. 'Remember, he was a highwayman.'

'All the better,' Emer said. 'I admire really dangerous men. They're always the most interesting and exciting.'

I had been sitting quietly beside Ita listening to the conversation and watching the waves ebb and flow as the tide slowly went out leaving great shining boulders, bands of dark golden sand and swathes of green-brown and emerald seaweed.

Then I heard Rowan say, 'Well, Nicola, do you agree with that?'

I glanced at him, startled by the suddenness of the

challenge. It was an attempt to embarrass me, I felt sure, and I determined not to let myself appear confused or at a loss. 'It all depends on what Emer means by dangerous,' I said slowly.

Emer shrugged. 'It's difficult to explain: it's a sort of quality some men have. They've either got it or they haven't, I suppose.'

'I don't think I've ever met any man with that quality,' I said.

Emer laughed shortly. 'Then you must have lived a singularly uneventful life. Surely in every woman's career there's one man whom she considers dangerous —to her peace of mind,' she added, glancing at me directly. 'Someone capable of disrupting her whole life and on whom her happiness hangs even if the man himself gives her no encouragement and is oblivious of the havoc he's creating in her heart.'

I reddened slightly. It was as though her fierce possessiveness of Rowan had made her acutely sensitive to any scent of rivalry from another woman. Had I betrayed myself to her by some look or glance, or was this simply a shot in the dark? I was aware that all eyes were fixed on me and managed to say lightly, 'As you say, my life has been uneventful.'

'Even since you came to Raheen?' she persisted.

'Well, today for instance, I was nearly drowned,' I replied dryly.

'And was rescued by Rowan, who happens to be the spit and image of the Black Delaney, so perhaps after all you're living more dangerously than you realize.'

I made some non-committal remark and after a moment Emer herself began a desultory conversation about the forthcoming auction in Galway. But I could see she was disappointed that she had not elicited a more revealing and satisfactory response. From what she was saying it was clear that she now had every intention of attending the auction, and neither Rowan nor Ita appeared the smallest bit surprised at this change of front.

Shortly after this we collected the remains of the picnic and fed the gulls that swept down in waves from the cliffs, their wings brilliant white in the light clear air. It was a relief to have something to do, for while Ita and Emer had been chatting, I had been conscious of Rowan watching me with a quizzical acuteness that I found extremely disturbing. When we had repacked the basket and shaken the sand out of our beach-shoes we began the climb up the steep path.

Emer forged ahead and stood laughing breathlessly at the top of the cliff as we straggled towards her, then flinging back her hair she shaded her eyes and gazed down on the rocks beneath. 'Well, look who's arrived on the scene,' she announced.

Then I saw, to my dismay, Brian Carbery's slim, slightly stooped figure leaning against the rocks and staring out to sea, just as I had seen him on my first visit to the cove.

I was uneasily conscious of the tension that had arisen between Ita and Rowan, although Emer seemed sublimely unaware of any change in the atmosphere.

'But how romantic, Ita! I hear all the other members of the archaeological party have gone home, so he must have stayed on just to moon around Raheen in the hope of catching a glimpse of you.'

'Does he realize he's trespassing on private property?'

Rowan's voice was deep with rage. He laid down the basket. 'I'll go down and tell him to clear off.'

I saw Ita's face whiten and guessed the misery she must endure if Rowan was to carry out his threat and brutally order from his property the man she had hoped to marry.

Emer watched him in silence as he prepared to descend, her apricot lips parted in anticipation and excitement, and I knew that she was actually looking forward to the confrontation between the two men. She was completely oblivious of the misery of the girl who stood beside her, pale and stricken, as she realized that no appeal would sway her brother from his course.

Before I was aware of what I was about to do I sprang forward and caught him by the arm. 'Don't, Rowan!' I shouted excitedly. 'Can't you see you'll do more harm than good? Ita has suffered enough. Do you want to leave her nothing—not even the knowledge that she's in his thoughts? How can you be so cruel?' I ended passionately. 'Can't you see how unhappy she is?'

An appalled silence followed this outburst. It was as though the wind that stirred the short stubby grasses was bearing my voice towards the sea in an eldritch shriek that merged with the calls of the gulls that swept high above the cliffs.

Rowan's eyes blazed down into mine as he roughly shook off my clutching hand. 'Stay out of this, Nicola! This has nothing to do with you.'

He spoke with measured savagery and I realized it was a warning, but, trembling with agitation, I was beyond all caution and tugged frantically at his sleeve with both hands.

For a moment he gazed at me in exasperation, then, suddenly catching me up in his arms, tossed me on to a bank of wild fuchsia.

Ita, losing her look of frozen misery, started forward. 'You've hurt her,' she said accusingly, and helped me to my feet.

As I rubbed ruefully at my ankle, he hesitated and turned. 'Are you all right?' he asked roughly.

Sensing that his attention was diverted from Brian Carbery, I continued rubbing vigorously at my ankle, although it had only been slightly bruised.

He frowned doubtfully. 'As far as I can see, you haven't been hurt.'

'Perhaps not,' I replied coldly, 'but my feelings have been hurt,' and I turned and walked away from him along the cliff path.

But before I had taken more than a few steps I heard his long strides following me. 'Don't be in such a hurry,' he growled as he caught up with me.

I turned and saw Emer standing beside the door of her low red car, a look of bewilderment on her face. 'But, Rowan,' she called, 'I was going to ask you to come back to Drumbeg.'

'Not today, Emer,' he answered, with a hint of irritation at the interruption.

With a look of outrage she got into the car and crashed the door shut.

Rowan turned back to me and said gruffly, 'On second thoughts perhaps I'd better carry you back to the house, just in case that ankle gives you trouble later.'

'That won't be necessary,' I answered stiffly, but as I turned away he swept me into his arms and despite my protests marched vigorously towards the Castle.

Ita caught up with us and glanced at me gratefully. My defence of Brian Carbery had proved to her that, far from being a spy, I was firmly on her side and that I was fully prepared to cross swords with her brother.

'What are you two grinning about?' he asked, as Ita hurried along beside us, keeping pace with his long strides.

'Oh, just that I'm glad you brought Nicola to Raheen,' she said ingenuously.

'And what about you?' He glanced down at me.

I was tempted to betray the happiness I felt in having his arms so close about me, but instead said demurely, 'I haven't been long enough at Raheen, or know you well enough, to tell.'

'Indeed! Then we must rectify that. I must see that in future we cultivate each other's acquaintance,' he said as we arrived at the orchard gate.

CHAPTER EIGHT

A SMALL man in a dusty bowler hat was standing outside O'Flanagan's auction-room dolefully swinging a handbell as we drove down the narrow Galway street.

'Do hurry, Derry,' Emer said impatiently. 'I want to get a chance of seeing the ring before the place becomes packed.'

Derry waited until he had manoeuvred past a young boy driving an ass which was drawing a cart laden with turnips. 'My dear girl, why didn't you tell me before? I could easily have mown down that young lad. I'm perfectly sure his family would be most sympathetic when they heard you were merely in a hurry to feast your beautiful optics on the Delaney ring.'

'There's no need to be sarcastic,' Emer said crossly, 'but you know what these places are like. Everyone stuck as close as sardines so that you can hardly even see what's up for sale.'

'Don't worry. When it comes to the Delaney ring you'll know all about it.'

'I do hope it's not bid up too high,' Emer fretted. 'It's the sort of thing that would probably attract the Dublin dealers.'

'It will hardly have much interest for anyone except the family,' Ita said reassuringly. 'After all, it's simply its history that makes it unique.'

'I do wish you had let Daddy have his way,' Emer said pettishly. 'It's stupid to be so proud and I think his suggestion was perfectly sensible under the circumstances——' She stopped awkwardly and fell silent and

I remembered that earlier, when we had called at Drumbeg to collect her, her father had not troubled to conceal his attitude.

As we drew up to the tall ugly grey house, gaunt and strictly utilitarian among its cement yards and rows of stabling, I had seen a short stout figure in riding breeches uncoupling a horse-box.

'I want you to meet Nicola,' Emer had called as she came out of the house, dressed in a trouser suit of mint green corduroy, a great floppy hat of tangerine felt almost obscuring her radiant hair.

She had glanced with disfavour at her father as he shook hands, his fingers rough with hard work, a friendly smile on his broad weather-beaten face. 'Really, Daddy, why don't you get the men to do the dirty work?' she said impatiently.

'Because, my girl, I have found that if I want a job done well I've got to do it myself,' he replied good-naturedly.

It had been obvious from his indulgent manner that he had often been over this ground with his daughter, and Emer had given an exclamation of exasperation as she got into the car and flopped down beside me.

Mr Lacey had leaned on the door and addressed Derry. 'I hear you're off today after this Delaney ring.'

Derry nodded. 'Rowan asked Ita to bid for it.'

Mr Lacey poked his head around the window and with a conspiratorial air said to Ita, 'If it goes too high for your pocket, remember you can count on me to make up the difference.'

I saw Ita glance at her brother in surprise and Derry's eyebrows had shot up in exaggerated bewilderment.

'But I don't understand,' Ita protested. 'Surely you don't mean you want to contribute to the price?'

He nodded with satisfaction. 'That's exactly what I do mean. Emer tells me it was used as a betrothal ring and when Rowan gets around to proposing it's the ring he'll give to my little girl, so naturally I'm keen you should keep it in the family.'

'I see,' Derry said softly. 'Well, I must congratulate you on your frankness, but it's completely out of the question that you should help to buy it. Not, mind you, that I give a damn myself, but Rowan would certainly never permit it. He's inclined to be touchy on such matters.'

Mr Lacey's friendly face had clouded. 'Do you think not? Well, perhaps you're right, but the man's too proud and standoffish for my taste.'

Later on I was to hear almost the same words echoed by the redoubtable Mrs Tarrant.

When Derry had parked the car in the courtyard of the Spanish Head, a small farmers' hotel where we were to have lunch, we went into the auction-room; now the clanging bell had stopped: people were beginning to trickle in, watched keenly by a large woman in rough brick-coloured tweeds. Her grey hair was cut in a chopped bob and she was seated on a Georgian writing-table swinging her stout legs, a small cigar between her large masculine fingers.

Immediately she saw us she waved and shouted, 'So you've come for that blackguard of an ancestor's ring, have you? I thought the news of the sale would flush you out all right, but where's Rowan? I expected him to arrive in person.'

Derry grinned, evidently well accustomed to the

lady's eccentricities. 'But I thought you didn't like Rowan.'

'Neither I do,' Mrs Tarrant snorted. 'I can't stand the man; proud as a peacock and arrogant as the devil; not my cup of tea at all.' She tapped the ash from her cigar on the toe of her heavy brogue shoe and fixed her choleric blue eyes on me. 'And who's the pretty girl? Come, man, introduce us.'

When Derry had amusedly done as she demanded, she said thoughtfully, 'So you're Nicola Fletcher! I've heard about you, but you're much prettier than I expected poor relations are usually so damnably ugly!' She turned her attention to Emer. 'Well, how do you like having a beauty like Nicola under the same roof with Rowan? If I were you I'd get hitched to him as soon as possible. Rowan, for all his high-and-mightiness, might be more susceptible than you think.'

'I haven't the remotest idea of what you're talking about,' Emer said tightly.

Mrs Tarrant chuckled. 'Haven't you? Listen, Emer Lacey, I've known you since you were a little chit of a thing, in pinafores, running about Drumbeg queening it over the stable lads, and I've seen you grow into a man-eater without a thought in your head for anything except your looks and what they can buy you in male attention. You're not the type to let a woman, especially a pretty one, poach on your preserves. I'll be interested to observe your tactics in disposing of the enemy.'

For the first time since my arrival at Raheen I saw Emer really disconcerted as she gazed in speechless fury at the older woman.

Ita said hurriedly, 'We'd better go in. Emer wants to

have a look at the ring before the room fills up.'

She had been hoping evidently to put an end to Mrs Tarrant's outrageous remarks and strategically withdraw, but she couldn't have chosen a more unfortunate subject.

'So you want to see the ring, Emer?' Mrs Tarrant guffawed. 'Yes, I'll bet you'd like to see it on the third finger of your left hand. Well, there's many a slip, as they say——'

With her face convulsed with fury Emer brushed past Mrs Tarrant, who crossed her stout legs and surveyed us from her perch like an outsize goblin as we scuttled past her in the wake of Emer.

Inside the auction-room we found groups of interested onlookers gathered about the glass cases which held the treasures of another age: hand-painted fans of ivory were displayed behind silver buckles: jewelcases of tortoiseshell and pearl, a quizzing glass set in an ornately chased silver mount and—looking oddly out of place—a child's simple coral necklace. There was also a selection of snuff-boxes in enamels, silver and gold, one of which had inset in its silver lid the initials 'N.F.' elaborately outlined in tiny amethysts.

When Ita noticed my interest she joined me and peered into the case and when she saw it gave an exclamation of surprise. 'Why, it has your initials, Nicola, and it's just the perfect shape for holding a lipstick!' She paused and glanced at me a little shyly. 'I only wish I could buy it for you.'

It was her way of expressing gratitude for my defence of Brian Carbery, I knew, and I was glad that the trinket, in its own way, had served to bring us closer together. I felt that her wish to obtain it for me was a step forward in our friendship, but I could think of nothing to say and there was a short awkward pause, broken by Derry, who joined us to point out that the Delaney ring was being displayed in a separate case.

As I stole a glance at Emer who was staring at it with avid intensity I began to understand her anxiety to possess it. Its appearance alone was striking: a great oval of pale celadon jade surrounded by a double border of tiny pearls and rubies; against the paleness of the jade the rubies flaming like drops of fire. I had never before taken much interest in jewellery or trinkets, but now for the first time I was keenly aware of what it would be to be the possessor of such a beautiful jewel.

Emer turned to Ita and said almost feverishly, 'Whatever happens you must buy it! If only Rowan weren't so pig-headed and would let Daddy help! I'll simply die if it falls to someone else!'

The morning dragged on with Emer showing little interest in the proceedings until the Delaney ring came up for sale. It was obvious that Ita had received instructions from Rowan to secure it at all costs, because in spite of strong competition she succeeded in having it knocked down to her. There was just time to fill in the cheque before the proceedings broke up for lunch.

There and then in the vast gloomy auction-room from which people were drifting in little gossiping groups of twos and threes, Emer took the ring from its dusty morocco case, thrust it on the third finger of her left hand and held it up so that the light could catch the pearls and rubies.

'When you've quite finished admiring it,' Derry said sarcastically, 'perhaps we could go for lunch.'

The small country hotel was a bustle of activity as we went along the narrow passage that led to the dining-room. On one side was the open door of the bar and as we passed I was hailed by Mrs Tarrant's familiar booming voice. 'Here, girl,' she called, 'I want a word with you.'

Inside at a small table, a glass of stout in one hand, and the familiar cigar in the other, sat Daisy Tarrant. 'No, not the rest of you,' she called peremptorily, as we paused, 'just the Fletcher girl! I want to talk to her privately without any snooping Delaney ears listening in. Too damned facetious, that's what's wrong with you, Derry.'

'You may as well humour the old girl,' Derry said in an undertone. 'We'll go on in and order for you.'

Reluctantly I entered the crowded bar. It was dense with cigarette smoke and a babel of voices rose above the clank of glasses as the Dublin dealers voraciously discussed the sale. Mrs Tarrant eyed me critically as I sat across from her at the small wooden table. 'And just what are you doing among the Delaneys, girl?' she asked abruptly. 'You're like a lamb among wolves.'

'I'm anything but a lamb,' I said flatly.

She gave a dry chuckle. 'So you're able to stick up for yourself! Just as well, for the Delaneys pride themselves on plain speaking.' She called over a passing waiter and ordered an orangeade. 'That's what I drank at your age,' she informed me firmly. 'Wait until you're as old and as hardbitten as I am before you touch anything stronger.'

'You also pride yourself on straight-speaking, don't

you?' I said as the waiter returned with a sweet vividly coloured orange concoction surmounted by two straws.

'Perhaps that's why there's no love lost between us,' she admitted. 'I can't stand Rowan's airs of damned superiority.'

'And Ita?' I asked a little dryly. 'Do you approve of her?'

She frowned at the tip of her cigar. 'The girl's one of those sullen introspective types that I've no patience with. What she needs is a husband, but she'll probably turn into a sour old spinster if Rowan gets his way.'

'What do you want to speak to me about?' I asked abruptly. To my own surprise I felt defensive about the Delaneys and found Mrs Tarrant's discussion of the state of affairs at Raheen distasteful and depressing.

She laid down her empty glass decisively. 'It struck me you might be glad of a job when the Delaneys kick you out!'

I gazed at her white-faced. Her brutal words had shocked and bewildered me.

'Oh, there's no need to look so surprised,' she said bluntly, 'for even if Rowan should feel a family attachment, Emer certainly won't. She's a jealous, green-eyed, vicious little she-devil, and she'll make it her business to see that she puts as much distance between you and Rowan as possible.'

I tried not to show the helpless misery I felt at her words.

'Huh,' she scoffed, 'do you think that Rowan Delaney is made of brass and that a pretty, fresh young girl underneath his roof has left him completely unmoved, because if you do you're in for a rude awakening.

Rowan is hot-blooded, like all the Delaneys—and no one should know that better than Emer.'

I made a pretence of sipping at the orange concoction, so that she would not see by my expression how near the mark she was. I remembered that passionate embrace in the moonlight and Ita's ambiguous reference to the scene she had overheard between Emer and Rowan.

'Look, girl,' her voice was gruffly gentle, 'what I'm trying to tell you is that any time you need a job come to Daisy Tarrant. It's not everyone I get along with, for I believe in speaking my mind without any soft soap, but I've a feeling that you'd be patient with me. Besides,' she added, 'I get lonely all by myself in that old place, but you mustn't ever tell anyone I said that.'

I stood up. 'Thanks, Mrs Tarrant, I'll think it over and if I ever need a job I'll certainly come to you.' Yet it was strange how remote I thought that eventually would be. As I left she was already calling friendly insults to a red-faced man in loud checks, and I could see they were old acquaintances.

When I joined the others in the dining-room a meal had been ordered.

Emer said casually, 'What did Daisy want to talk to you about? We're gasping to know.'

I felt a temptation to say—she spoke of you and the fact that you will in all probability fling me out when you are mistress of Raheen.

'You mean *you're* gasping to know,' Derry contradicted. 'Don't tell her, Nicola. It's absolutely none of her business.'

'I didn't intend to,' I said quietly.

Derry raised his brows quizzically. 'My, haven't we

128

become very strong-minded and uppish? Not at all the correct attitude for the poor relation!'

But it was impossible to be angry or offended by even his most outrageous remarks. I smiled without retorting and Emer shrugged with a show of indifference.

'Oh, keep your silly secrets, if you want to! Actually I'd say she's been trying to pump you about the Delaneys—and getting in a few snide remarks about horrid Emer Lacey. Of course she detests me thoroughly, just because I don't take her insolence without hitting back.'

She was sitting facing the door and I saw her face brighten as it swung open. 'Here's Rowan. So he's turned up after all!'

I could see she regarded his arrival as a triumph and she twisted the ring excitedly on her finger as he approached.

As soon as he joined us she waved her left hand teasingly before his face. 'Well, what do you think of it?' she demanded triumphantly.

Against Emer's long slim fingers the ring was displayed to superb advantage and for a long moment he followed the flickering undulations of her hand. I was uncomfortably aware of a stiffening in his manner and wondered that she had not detected it too.

But she was so completely absorbed in her new acquisition that she was oblivious of the change in atmosphere. 'Isn't it utterly gorgeous, Rowan? You must let me wear it and not put it in that stuffy old safe in your office. Anyway, it's just my fit and I'd simply loathe to part with it now.'

'But I'm afraid that's exactly what you'll have to do,'

he said evenly. 'As you know, it's the family betrothal ring and it shall be reserved for that purpose.'

Emer paled and bit her lip as she caught the malicious glint in Derry's eyes at this rebuff, then, with an awkward laugh, she pulled it from her finger. 'Oh, there's your old ring, if you're going to be so stuffy about it!' And she dropped it into his outstretched palm. But I could see that her attitude was that it was a ridiculous formality, when it was only a matter of time before she would be in full possession of it. 'Why did you bother to come when you only intended to make yourself unpleasant?' she asked tightly.

'I can assure you I had no intention of coming to Galway today, but a piece of machinery broke down, and I had no choice in the matter.'

It was plain that she took the admission that he had not come in response to her imperious demands as a further humiliation and relapsed into sulky silence.

For once, however, Ita was impervious to her friend's change of mood and chatted with unusual animation about the articles for sale at the auction— including the snuff-box with the jewelled initials 'N.F.'

For an instant Rowan glanced at me as she commented on the coincidence, then he seemed to become abstracted and I got the impression that he was not paying much attention to his sister's chatter. He left us immediately after lunch and Emer, who had preserved a frozen silence since parting with the ring, announced curtly that she wanted to go home.

'But I'd planned to do some shopping,' Ita protested, then as she saw Emer's stormy expression, said disappointedly, 'Oh well, if you're determined, I suppose I can wait until another time.' But I could see that she was, for once, faintly intolerant of Emer's self-willed decisions.

On the drive back Emer's mood was in marked contrast to the excited anticipation she had shown when we had set out, and when we dropped her at the gates of Drumbeg, her manner was distinctly unfriendly.

Derry breathed a sigh of relief when she had left the car. 'Thank heavens! I had the feeling she was going to invite herself back and I couldn't really bear any more of it! I pity Rowan if he's fool enough to take her, because she'll definitely make his life a misery.'

'I imagine it would be hard to make Rowan's life a misery,' Ita said dryly. 'He specializes in that himself! Anyway, why did he not let Emer wear the ring? After all, when she becomes officially engaged to him, she'll have it anyway.'

Derry laughed. 'Perhaps he's waiting for the right setting—a warm summer evening with a full moon and the scent of roses, and Emer in a glamorous dress with the love-light in her eye. It's fairly obvious she's as hard as nails, though! Imagine bestowing on yourself an old and romantic ring in the middle of an auction-room! It certainly looks as if her main interest is in becoming mistress of Raheen.'

'But then you were always prejudiced against her!' Ita said thoughtfully, but she spoke with a certain detachment; no longer with the fierce partisanship that probably stemmed from her own resentment against her brother.

'Well, thank heavens she didn't honour us with her company tonight,' Derry said as we drove through the gates of Raheen. He glanced at the lowering clouds that were gathered in dark sullen columns above the sea. 'It looks as if there's a bad storm blowing up and I certainly wouldn't relish driving her back to Drumbeg.'

To me the thick enfolding walls of the Castle, instead of appearing forbidding, seemed protective and sheltering, but as the afternoon passed and there was no sign of Rowan, I found it difficult to hide my restlessness and occasionally I would pull back the thick curtains of the cosy sitting-room in which we sat and peer out. Through the slanting rain I could see the trees writhing in the fierce wind that had arisen and howled about the Castle.

'You're not worrying about Rowan, are you?' Derry asked slyly.

I let the curtains fall and turned with an air of indifference. 'Just watching the storm: there's something so wild and elemental about it: it's frightening, yet fascinating to a suburban like myself.' But I had the feeling that he was not deceived.

'This is mild compared to what it will be later. But don't worry. Rowan's not out there, dying of exposure. He has probably stopped at Drumbeg on the way home and made it up with Emer: I'd say he finds it hard to be at odds with her, even though he may despise himself for it—but then she's that sort of woman.'

'Oh yes, of course, he probably stopped at Drumbeg,' I said flatly. But it was something I hadn't thought of! No quarrel is lasting when people are in love: I should have remembered that. What a fool I'd been to have been anxiously watching at the window when he was probably at that very moment in Emer's arms and she was once more the possessor of the Delaney ring!

Later on as the three of us sat near a blazing wood fire, the thick hangings muting the howl of the wind and the lashing rain, I began to feel a warm glow of belonging. Ita's manner was friendly and even Derry's cynical comments were toned down as though in answer to an unspoken appeal.

Afterwards, when Derry had taken himself off, Ita and I sat beside the fire chatting quietly, but we were both sleepy after the long drive and retired early.

It had been easy to forget the storm while I was with the others, but once I was alone in my own room I was uneasily aware of the sound of the waves dashing against the cliff and the banshee screams of the wind as it howled about the jutting wings and crenellated roofs of Raheen.

Before getting into bed I crossed to the window and gazed out: greenish-black clouds scudded across the blurred lustreless moon and the black foliage in the avenue bent and writhed as though in some lurid witches' dance: then suddenly I was aware of a darker shadow that detached itself from the contortions of the shrubbery and moved closer to the house. My heart thudded with unreasoning terror as I saw a wide enveloping garment billow up like a great wing and obscure the tall approaching figure. Then dark clouds scurried across the sky, blotting out everything in impenetrable darkness.

I let the curtains drop and stood shivering, half in cold, but mostly in the icy grip of dread. Could it be possible that Doreen was right? Had I seen the apparition of the Black Delaney that she insisted was haunting the avenue?

With clammy hands I shrugged into a warm dressing-gown. Doreen, I knew, intended spending the night at the Castle, partly because of the storm but partly because her sense of duty would not allow her to return to the lodge until Rowan was safely home and she had seen him provided with a hot meal. I would go down to the kitchen, I decided, and ask her for coffee and perhaps fetch a book before returning to my room. No doubt by that time I would have banished the ridiculous panic that clutched at my limbs and made me scurry down the staircase anxious for the warmth and light of the kitchen.

I found Doreen comfortably seated in a wooden rocker by the range, her ample figure supported by chintz cushions, a cup and saucer by her side. A fire of red coals glowed through the bars and an old-fashioned coffee pot stood at the back of the range, filling the kitchen with the delicious fragrance.

She looked up in surprise from the sock she was darning. 'Why, Miss Nicola, whatever brings you here at this time of night—and you as white as a sheet!' She snipped off a thread, carefully withdrew a pink wooden darning mushroom and laid the sock in an overflowing sewing-basket. 'Anyone would think by the look of you that you'd seen a ghost—the Black Delaney, no doubt,' she added with a chuckle. 'Then people would be more ready to believe me instead of acting like I was imagining everything.'

'I expect it was the sound of the sea lashing against the cliffs and the howl of the wind,' I said evasively. I could well imagine her reactions were I to tell her I thought I had glimpsed the apparition of the Black Delaney!

'Oh, you'll get well used to it in time,' she said comfortably, and glanced a little anxiously at the clock. 'I can't imagine what's keeping Mr Rowan it's not often he's as late as this.'

Her words renewed all my earlier anxiety about Rowan. Suppose he had met with an accident and was lying badly injured somewhere on a bleak deserted road? I gave a little shiver of apprehension and Doreen got to her feet with an exclamation.

'You're perished with the cold! A nice cup of coffee will heat you up in no time.' She took the pot from the range and filled up a cup with steamy black coffee. 'Help yourself to cream and sugar, dearie,' she said kindly, 'and sit here by the fire until you warm up.'

We sat in comfortable silence as I sipped it and she nodded good-naturedly when at last I laid down the cup. As I left she said softly, 'Don't fret about Mr Rowan. He'll find his way home safe and sound, never fear.'

I went back to the sitting-room where earlier I had noticed some magazines of Ita's strewn on an armchair. The light from the dying embers of the fire filled the room with a shadowed and ruddy glow and glinted off the dark gilt of the pictures. The thick old sheepskin rug in front of the fire looked warm and inviting. I collected a few of the glossy magazines that had been tossed carelessly on the wide chintz-covered easy-chair and then hesitated. Snug beside the fire I could wait until I heard Rowan return then, once sure of his safety, I could slip upstairs unseen.

It was at this moment that I heard a movement in the room and with a scream of alarm I dropped the magazines and swung around. A tall figure was loung-ing negligently in one of the deep comfortable armchairs. 'Rowan!' I quavered.

'Well, who did you think it was?' he asked in amusement.

'It could have been the Black Delaney,' I said crossly. 'I've come to the conclusion that in this old place almost anything could happen. I'm certain I saw someone in the avenue and he seemed to be wearing a cloak, although I didn't dare tell Doreen in case she went into hysterics.'

'Just as well you didn't,' he said calmly, as he bent forward and tossed a log on to the fire, 'for the bogey man you saw was me. The car broke down near the lodge gates and I put one of Thady's old-fashioned coats about my shoulders and walked up.'

'Oh,' I said, feeling slightly foolish. Then, to cover up my embarrassment, I bent down to collect the scattered magazines. 'Well, why didn't you let me know you were here before now?'

'Because I wanted to watch you.'

The calm effrontery of this admission left me speechless. Then I said inanely, 'But—but why? I was simply looking for something to read.'

'Was that all? I saw you look towards the window and listen to the storm, then glance back at the fire as though you were reluctant to return to your room. Are you lonely there, all by yourself in that vast old room?'

I seized on this explanation eagerly: far better he should think that I was childishly nervous than know I had been considering keeping a vigil for his return! 'The rooms are so big and old I suppose they are inclined to make one's imagination run riot,' I said.

There was a long pause and my voice seemed to hang on the air. He had turned towards the fire and it was impossible to see the expression on his face and for a moment I wondered if he had been listening to me. Without looking at me, he said gently, 'Won't you stay here with me for a while, Nicola? There's something I want to tell you.'

Even if I had wanted to, it would have been impossible to resist the appeal in his voice. This was a Rowan I had never experienced before.

As I was about to sit in the armchair, he said, 'No, not there! Here, beside me.'

Slowly I crossed and stood in front of him and holding out his hands he took mine in his and gently pulled me on to the thick rug so that my shoulders were resting against him. 'Now you're not frightened any more, are you?' His hand gently caressed my hair.

I shook my head. It was stupid to feel so much happiness, I told myself. After all, the gesture was no more than one of kindness to a newcomer unused to the vast and gloomy rooms of Raheen.

'I've heard of a surgeon who specializes in the kind of operation Ita needs,' he began. 'It's essential, of course, that he sees her before any decision can be made. However, I can see she likes and trusts you and I have great hopes that you will be able to persuade her to discuss the matter with him. You'll do your best, won't you, Nicola?'

I found myself feeling suddenly deflated. So his kindness had been simply a preliminary to asking my co-operation in persuading his sister to consult a plastic surgeon! Foolish tears of disappointment filled my eyes and I gazed stolidly at the fire in an effort to keep them from overflowing. After all, I told myself fiercely, I should be delighted that I could be of use to

Ita and her brother: it would give me a purpose in the household.

His fingers closed about my chin and forced me reluctantly to face him. 'Tears,' he said, 'but why? Do you dislike Ita? I know she can be singularly unpleasant when she likes.'

'It's not that. I like her and I think she likes me a little. It's just——' But it was impossible to explain what I felt to this man.

'You gave me to understand very clearly when you first come that you wanted to be of use. Well, here's your chance.'

The fire sputtered up a shower of sparks and I could see the mockery that glittered in his eyes.

'It's late: I must go,' I said, unable to control the quiver in my voice.

I was about to get to my feet, but his hands on my shoulders pushed me down. 'No, we mustn't part at odds with each other, Nicola. Anyway, I have another purpose in asking you to stay.' He felt in his pocket and produced a tiny oval tissue-wrapped package. 'Open it,' he urged.

But even before I unfastened the white tissue I guessed what it contained and my heart thumped ridiculously with excitement and pleasure. 'So you bought it, after all,' I whispered, as the little snuff-box lay in my hand, my initials in jewels glittering in the firelight.

'Now are we friends?' he asked dryly, 'and I assure you that this is not an attempt at bribery and corruption!'

'It's beautiful,' I answered, 'and I'll try to persuade Ita to do as you wish, although I'll probably not succeed. She's so determined not to give an inch.'

He grimaced. 'I'm afraid that's a family failing! On the whole I think Derry's the most easy-going of us—too easy-going, I'm afraid, at times. By the way,' he added slowly, 'he hasn't been bothering you, has he?'

I looked at him in surprise. 'What do you mean?'

'He has the reputation of being a local Casanova. I'd hate to think he was making a nuisance of himself.' He hesitated. 'I expect you know what I mean.'

So my dark forceful Rowan was actually shy of putting his fears into words, I thought gleefully.

I leaned my head against his knee and smiled demurely into the fire. 'No, of course not. I expect I'm really not his type,' I said dreamily.

Rowan's arm was about my shoulder and the only interest I felt in Derry was a vague gratitude that he had been the cause of Rowan's concerning himself about my welfare. But I was not to know how soon I would have good cause to take Derry Delaney much more seriously.

CHAPTER NINE

DURING the night the storm blew itself out. The next day was calm and the sky and grounds had the clean-swept look that follows a high wind. The rotting rusty leaves were swept into great piles beneath the bare trees and the walls of the Castle had a chill glitter in the pale wintery light. It was much too cold for bathing, but later when I went down to the cove I found it had a wild beauty of its own: kelp was strewn on the pebbles and debris from the sea had been washed up to the mouth of the cave. The breakers curled on the sands leaving bands of white spume. I wandered about the cove for a time revelling in the tangy salt air and searching among the wrack for stones worn and polished by the storm into things of beauty.

It was later when I had climbed the cliff path that I once again glimpsed Brian Carbery. He was walking swiftly, hands in pockets, along the narrow tufted path that edged the cliff and staring out to sea. I waved to him and turned to continue the path that led towards the orchard gate. There was something about the thin haunched figure that gave me the impression he was not in the mood to exchange civil chatter.

But as I moved away he hastened his steps and called out, 'Hello there! I'd like to talk to you, Miss Fletcher, if you're not in a hurry.'

'I'm never in a hurry at Raheen,' I said, 'in fact I haven't enough to do to keep me busy.'

'Lucky you,' he smiled. 'Now in my case it's usually

the direct opposite. However, I'll be leaving here soon for a rest before setting off next season for Crete. I've been invited to join an expedition there.'

'You're leaving?' I exclaimed in dismay. Somehow I had always felt that sooner or later there would be the possibility of his coming to an understanding with Ita. It was hard to believe that soon the cove would be empty for ever of his long scholarly figure leaning against the rocks thoughtfully smoking his pipe.

Now that he was near me I saw the lines of strain about his eyes. What had persuaded him at last that Ita was lost to him? I wondered. 'But why?' I asked impulsively. 'I thought——'

'You thought I was going to hang around indefinitely: was that it?' he asked ruefully. 'Well, perhaps I might have, if I hadn't seen that there's no future in it. I thought at one time that if I waited long enough I might get Ita to see my point of view, but I realize now it's hopeless. She's much too completely under Rowan's thumb. It was pretty obvious, that day on the cliff: she didn't even turn her head. I knew then that I didn't stand a chance. It's clear that I'm only an embarrassment to her now, and the sooner I'm off the better. The only thing I regret is that she never saw the dig. I felt so sure that she would have been interested——'

'You must show it to her before you go,' I said impulsively.

'Do you really think she'd agree?' he asked eagerly.

I hesitated, regretting my officiousness. How would Rowan react if he heard that I had been instrumental in bringing his sister and Brian Carbery together again, even on such an innocent expedition as viewing the dig?

'We can't talk here,' he said. 'Won't you let me drive you into Galway and we could discuss things over a cup of coffee?'

I nodded reluctantly, wishing I could extricate myself without hurting him too much.

As we drove towards Galway I was relieved to find that he kept the conversation to strictly neutral subjects, but once inside the Spanish Head I found myself listening miserably as he made detailed plans for the following afternoon. Only a few people sat in the rather dingy old-fashioned room with its gloomy green-painted walls. A small coke fire in the iron grate barely took the chill from the damp air and I wished heartily that I had not met him on the cliff top and made the impulsive suggestion. Before I quite knew how he had done it I found myself agreeing to bring Ita to the dig on the following afternoon, and I realized that in spite of his gentleness Brian Carbery had a dangerously persuasive charm.

Gradually, however, my reluctance must have penetrated, because he said a little wistfully, 'You're not regretting anything, are you, or are you as much under Rowan Delaney's thumb as his sister is?'

The question made me instantly defensive. 'No, of course not!' But in spite of my denial I had the uneasy feeling of not being strictly truthful. Suppose Rowan were to find out that his sister and I had visited the dig as guests of Brian Carbery he would instantly realize that I must have had a hand in it, and the memory of those sweet moments by the fire made me reluctant to risk his disapproval.

I felt wretchedly indecisive as I listened to Brian happily plan how he would get the small hut beside the dig tidied up and refreshments supplied for our visit. It was obviously going to be for him a great and happy occasion and I realized that, although he hadn't even hinted at it, he had hopes of convincing Ita of his love for her. I wished fervently that I were anywhere but in this dingy room with its prevailing smell of boiled greens, and breathed a sigh of relief when at length we regained the street and made our way towards Brian's parked car. But my relief was short-lived, for as we were walking side by side on the narrow pavement, Brian elated and talkative, a car approached from the opposite direction. As it passed it slowed to a crawl and I happened to glance idly at its driver, then felt my heart stand still as I saw that the man behind the wheel was Rowan.

He glanced with stony deliberation from one to the other of us, then accelerated and drove swiftly past.

Sick with misery and apprehension, I slipped into the seat beside Brian.

'That was Rowan, wasn't it?' he asked without particular curiosity. 'I thought I recognized that obstinate dark jaw of his: it looked, from his expression, as if he strongly objected to you even being seen in my company. What a bully the man is! I'm glad you've decided to take a stand against him or he'd probably end by ruining your life as he tried to ruin Ita's and my own.'

Strangely enough it was these words that made me realize beyond doubt that I loved Rowan Delaney. It was possible for him to ruin my life, of course—but only by sentencing me to separation from him. In spite of this knowledge I felt a resentment that I was, after all, so thoroughly in his power and I dreaded the com-

143

ing interview when I returned to the Castle, yet with typical feminine inconsistency I felt the urge to defend him to Brian who, I knew, regarded him merely as an arbitrary and domineering tyrant. 'I really believe Rowan thought he was acting for the best,' I said hesitantly, 'as far as Ita and yourself were concerned. You see, he still looks on Ita as his young and inexperienced sister. I expect he thought he was protecting her from someone more worldly and experienced.'

'Now you're being tactful, aren't you?' he commented dryly. 'You're telling me in the nicest way possible that Rowan thought I was a cynical adventurer, ready to take advantage of his sister's infatuation. Methinks you're springing to his defence with suspicious alacrity! Can it be that you're more involved with the man than you realize?'

I flushed and glanced away and he took his hand off the wheel and patted mine with avuncular solicitude. 'Sorry, I didn't mean to be nasty, but you can hardly expect me to feel particularly sympathetic towards the man. However, I can't tell you how pleased I am that you've agreed to go through with tomorrow's affair.' He hesitated, then added softly, 'It may make all the difference to our lives.'

And to mine too, I thought dismally, when he left me at the lodge gates and with a wave of his hand turned and drove back towards the village.

To my relief there was no sign of Rowan's car when I reached the Castle: whatever he had to say to me was to be postponed until he returned from the mines.

I found Ita in one of the small rooms near the kitchen where she was rather haphazardly sticking transparent covers on pots of marrow and ginger jam.

'Oh, hello.' She looked up and pushed the straight black hair from her forehead. 'Whatever became of you? We began to wonder if you'd gone bathing after all and got into difficulties, but Thady reported that he'd seen you drive off in a car. He wasn't near enough to identify the driver and was much chagrined. I expect he's afraid he's losing his touch as chief informer to the House of Delaney,' she added dryly.

I hesitated, then decided to take the bull by the horns. 'I'm just as glad he didn't, Ita, for I'd much rather you heard from me. It was Brian Carbery who drove me to Galway to discuss the possibility of your going with me to see the dig.'

'Oh!' Ita bent her head and slapped another cover on a jar. 'Of course you must know it's completely out of the question,' she said unequivocally.

I felt my heart sink. Far from simply discussing the problem I had actually undertaken to bring Ita to the dig on the following day. I had a quick mental picture of Brian Carbery, his handsome face quietly elated as he busily prepared the hut for the reception of his fair lady.

'But what difference would it make now?' I asked. 'He's leaving. Next year he's going on an expedition to Crete.'

'Leaving?' Ita straightened, her eyes wide with distress.

'Yes, leaving. Did you think he was going to hang around the cove for ever, gazing up at your bower window and hoping you'd smile on him, like a lovesick knight in a fairy-tale?' I asked with deliberate crudeness.

'Somehow I didn't think of him leaving for good,'

she said tonelessly.

'But he is, and you'd give him immense pleasure if you'd agree to visit the dig before he goes. He's so proud of his work and anxious to show it to someone he loves.'

'Someone he loves,' she repeated shakily. 'That sounds lovely, Nicola.'

'You're a very lucky girl,' I continued robustly. 'Not many men would have stuck it out so patiently, but even Brian has a breaking point and he has come to the conclusion that he's an embarrassment to you and that, as he's an embarrassment, he'd better leave, once and for all.'

'An embarrassment?' Ita wailed. 'Oh, how could he think that? He knows the reason why I thought it better we shouldn't meet again. I've always loved him and I think I always shall.' And quite suddenly and without warning she burst into floods of tears.

I had never seen Ita lose control completely before and for a moment I was stunned into silence. Then seizing meanly on the sign of weakening I said, 'All right, in that case visit him tomorrow and give him some happiness for a change, will you?'

Speechlessly she nodded.

'Very well,' I said briskly, 'in that case I'll go down to the village and ring him and tell him to expect us.'

She blew her nose with an air of finality and began to stack the pots on a slate shelf with a happy alacrity that was in complete contrast to her usual sullen reserve. 'You can phone from the hall,' she offered eagerly.

I shook my head. 'This time we mustn't have any

spies running to Rowan and spoiling things.'

'That's true. Thady is always lurking around the house. There's nothing he'd like better than to report it to Rowan.'

All the same I felt uneasy as I slipped down to the village post-office and phoned Brian.

He sounded touchingly happy. 'I needn't tell you I'm placing great hopes on being able to make her see things my way. Dear Nicola, thank you for playing Cupid.'

I put down the receiver, a hollow feeling in my stomach. By playing Cupid, as Brian put it, had I destroyed the frail tentative understanding that had slowly evolved between Rowan and myself? By the time I got back to the Castle, Rowan, more than likely, would have returned from work and I dreaded the interrogation that I knew would ensue. Somehow or other I must avoid giving away our plans.

When I reached the tall iron gates of Raheen I found them shut and knew Rowan must have returned. I entered by the green postern gate set into the wall. Thady, who was digging in the small garden that adjoined the lodge, didn't contribute to my peace of mind. He looked up on my approach and, resting on his spade, said with an air of deep satisfaction, 'Mr Rowan's after coming home and it looks as if he's lighting. Now I wonder what could be vexing him?' He smiled wolfishly and watched me closely, and I wondered if my nervous apprehension showed all too clearly.

'Of course you could never tell what would vex Mr Rowan, for he's a mighty hot-tempered man and flares up at the drop of a hat. It's often he's had good reason for flying off the handle—like the time that fellow Carbery that's digging up the countryside took a fancy to Miss Ita, and her, poor silly girl, got into her head she'd run off with him, and him, no doubt, only after her fortune! Well, Mr Rowan put a stop to that and I'd say now he'd be real annoyed if he thought Mr Carbery was hanging around, trying maybe to get friendly again with Miss Ita.'

His eyes narrowed slyly and I knew then that he had seen me return from Galway in Brian's car.

I had intended to ignore his insolence and walk on, but in spite of myself, I said angrily, 'If you hadn't spied on Miss Ita and told Mr Rowan of her plans, she'd probably have been happily married by now.'

To my surprise he looked genuinely bewildered. 'Tell Mr Rowan about Miss Ita! Sure devil a bit did I know she was planning to run off with the gentleman! Oh no, you've got me wrong there, miss! It was Miss Emer as told on her, for I heard her with me own two ears, so I did, and if anyone says different they're liars, so they are!'

With an air of conscious virtue he resumed his digging and I continued up the avenue. So I had been right in supposing Emer had informed Rowan of Ita's plans!

When I reached the Castle there was no sign of life in the hall and I tried to slip quietly up to my room, but any idea I might have had of escaping an interview with Rowan was dismissed by Doreen who appeared when I was halfway up the stairs.

Her usually good-natured face was troubled. 'Oh, Miss Nicola, Mr Rowan told me to say he wants to see you in the small parlour as soon as you came in.'

'Oh!' I hesitated and ran my fingers over the carving of the banister. 'Well, tell him I'll see him when I've taken my things off.'

She looked surprised and I thought faintly affronted at this off-hand treatment of her employer, but I was determined not to let her see how nervous I felt.

I went to my room, leisurely brushed my hair and tied it back with a gilt buckle, then, straightening the lace collar and cuffs that helped to take the drabness from my plain crêpe dress, I went downstairs. The little delay would show Rowan Delaney I was not intimidated by his peremptory orders, I thought with satisfaction.

The small parlour was a tiny room which seemed to be set into the thick walls like a cosy secret chamber. When I opened the door I found Rowan standing impatiently in front of the fire. He stared at me stonily. 'Did you get Doreen's message?'

'Yes,' I answered calmly. 'She told me as soon as I came in.'

He looked at his watch. 'Which was exactly a quarter of an hour ago.'

'I tidied up first,' I said with an air of carelessness.

He glanced briefly at my smoothly groomed hair. 'So I see, but I assure you it wasn't necessary. What I have to say to you has nothing whatever to do with your appearance. It concerns your association with Brian Carbery: I thought I had made my attitude towards the man perfectly plain when you came here! What do you mean by deliberately flouting my wishes?'

'And I also thought I had made it clear that I had no intention of allowing you to bully and dominate me,' I answered.

He looked faintly startled at my retort and I realized I must have been successful in hiding my nervousness. Then his face darkened. It was not often Rowan Delaney was met with such resistance from his minions. 'When it comes to Brian Carbery I have every right to interfere,' he grated. 'The man is a philanderer and obviously you've fallen for him every bit as heavily as my sister did. It was quite plain from your manner that you're completely infatuated. You were hanging on his words as though you were listening to the oracle. The very fact that he has turned his charm on you proves my point: any young girl is fair game for him, and the sillier the better!'

I was so startled by the accusation that I stared at him in open-mouthed astonishment. That he would accuse me of acting as go-between for Ita and Brian I had been certain, but I had not dreamed he would accuse me of a romantic interest in Brian. It had come as a complete surprise. Brian himself had made it so unflatteringly clear that my only function was that of playing Cupid, as he put it.

He regarded me in silence for a moment, then as I opened my mouth to retort said sarcastically, 'Why did he drive you to Galway? Was it to discuss the weather and the crops?'

I hesitated as I realized I had been on the verge of betraying Ita.

'I notice you don't answer,' he said dryly. 'No doubt you find it difficult to explain how you've become so friendly with a man whom you evidently met lurking about the grounds. Well, you'd better understand that I don't intend to permit you to carry on a flirtation with Brian Carbery. You must not see him again. Do I make myself plain?'

'How dare you!' I spluttered. 'Do you think you can behave like some sort of tyrant and dictate whom I may speak to just because you're the Delaney of Raheen? Well, I can assure you, as far as I'm concerned, you're very much mistaken!'

'Bravo! My sentiments exactly!'

I swung around to find Derry leaning against the doorway, clapping his hands in applause. I had no idea how long he had been there and, in spite of my anger against Rowan, Derry was the last person I would have wished to overhear our quarrel. His open contempt and cynicism made me distrust him and I guessed he would not hesitate to turn another's weaknesses to his own advantage.

'The lady's right, you know, Rowan,' he said. 'You're positively feudal in your views. Just because you're boss of the Delaney outfit you think you can dictate to all and sundry! Well, Nicola's not a Delaney—or at least not so bad one would notice it,' he added with a grin.

'Get out,' Rowan said tersely.

'Not until I've said my little piece. For your information I have applied for a position in Dublin. I admit the job is not exactly congenial: however, the fact that it will enable me to leave Raheen more than makes up for its deficiencies. I only wish I'd had the energy to get out ages ago.'

'I've a feeling you'll not be in your new job very long, if you run true to form,' Rowan told him. 'However, when you find yourself at a loose end again there will always be a place for you in the business.'

'Thanks,' Derry sneered, 'but I don't think I'll take

you up on the offer. I can imagine what life will be like in the old homestead when you get around to marrying Emer.'

I waited for a moment for Rowan's retort, then, as he made no effort to repudiate Derry's statement, I crept out of the room and realized that neither of them had noticed my departure.

When I reached my room I went to the window and gazed unseeingly over the grounds. It had begun to rain again: not the usual misty veil of moisture that would leave the grass emerald green and make all the autumn colours brightly vivid, but a heavy downpour that drummed on the window panes and blotted out the view. I could hear the raindrops hiss and splutter on the blazing logs in the wide chimney.

I glanced around my room with new eyes. In spite of its vast and ugly furniture I had come to regard it as my own. Here I was in my own particular niche in the scheme of things and it had given me a feeling of stability: I was used to the way the light glinted off the bevelled edge of the cheval mirror; to the flowered china toilet set on the dressing-table with the glass candlesticks on either side in their tiny crimson silk shades: even the creak of the wardrobe door had become familiar.

But when Rowan married Emer all would be changed: I knew her taste well enough to know that the old-world charm that I loved would be replaced by modern furniture and labour-saving devices. I had heard her speak disparagingly of the draughty old fireplaces and of the advantages of central heating. When she became mistress of Raheen she would see that I was removed and I felt a cold desolation sweep over me—yet what had I expected? Why had I allowed myself to be lulled into a sense of security just because Rowan one evening had shown a passing consideration and interest in me?

I hadn't realized I was crying until Ita put her head into the half-open doorway and said commiseratingly, 'Poor Nicola! Derry tells me you and Rowan had a fearful quarrel, but you mustn't let him upset you.'

'I'm not really upset,' I quavered, mopping my eyes. 'It's simply that I'm not used to such scenes, I suppose.'

She came into the room and nodded sympathetically. 'No, I expect when you lived with your aunt things were much more orderly and civilized. You must hate it here.'

I shook my head. 'No, I didn't hate it. Perhaps I was beginning to like it too well!'

She looked at me in puzzlement. 'What do you mean?'

'Just that I'm not prepared for the changes that are bound to take place when your brother marries Emer.'

She frowned and wandered over to the cheval mirror and looked at her reflection thoughtfully. 'Yes, I hadn't thought of that.'

'I imagine one of her first changes will be letting me know there's no place for me at Raheen.'

'You don't like Emer, do you?'

'No,' I said bluntly, 'but perhaps I'm prejudiced.'

Again she studied her reflection in abstracted silence. 'You know, Nicola, lately it has occurred to me that Emer and Rowan, if they marry, will lead a dog's life together: they're each so set on getting their own way. Sometimes I wonder if she really loves him, or is it simply that she's determined to conquer him as she does every man she meets?'

I knew I shouldn't ask the question, yet I couldn't prevent myself. 'Do you think Rowan is in love with her, Ita?'

She looked at me in surprise. 'What do you mean? I should think it's fairly obvious that he thinks her very beautiful. Most men do.'

'But apart from her looks, does he love her, as Brian loves you, I wonder, just because she is herself?'

She considered this. 'No, I can't imagine him hanging around Drumbeg if Emer should show signs of cooling off, but then she's never made any secret of the fact that she wants Rowan and is determined to get him. But why do you ask? You're not in love with him yourself, are you?' she asked bluntly.

Her gaze was direct and searching and I knew that there was no point in trying to deny it, for my secret would be safe with her.

I nodded. 'Not at the beginning when I first met him! I think I hated him then: he was so cold and arrogant all I could think of was trying to get away from him.' I laughed shakily. 'I know it's contradictory and doesn't make a bit of sense, but suddenly for no reason at all everything seemed to be different.'

She paused and said with a frankness that was characteristic, 'I do wish you hadn't fallen for him, for I think he will marry Emer. Fundamentally I imagine he's hypnotized by her beauty, although he's always trying to show her that she has no hold over him.'

I nodded and smiled ruefully. 'That's why I have to go, Ita.'

'Go? Oh, Nicola, you can't mean it!'

She sounded so distressed that my heart warmed to

her. 'You wouldn't want me to hang on here, eating my heart out for a man who looks on me as a sort of retainer, living in the shadow of his castle walls as it were?'

'But I shall miss you so dreadfully,' she said in dismay. 'Where will you go? Rowan could easily fix it so that no one around these parts would give you a job if he felt you should stay on here. He can be pretty ruthless when he wants to, as you know.'

'Yes, I know. But Daisy Tarrant doesn't like him.' I smiled wryly. 'She considers him too proud and aloof and altogether too overbearing. In fact all the faults I used to dislike him for! Actually she offered me a job that day we went to the auction in Galway, although at the time I didn't take her proposition particularly seriously.'

Ita smiled. 'But then no one takes Daisy particularly seriously. By the way, perhaps I should tell you that she has the reputation of being a bit too free and easy. Occasionally she throws parties at that weird house of hers and it seems the proceedings are pretty wild and uninhibited, so don't say I didn't warn you!'

'I imagine I'll be able to take care of myself,' I said firmly. 'Anyway, it's the only place I know of at present.'

'You're not going immediately?' she asked anxiously.

'Of course not,' I answered. 'We're to meet Brian tomorrow.'

At the time I thought our arrangements were to go according to plan—but then I was not to know what the night would bring.

It was still raining when I went to bed and for a long while I lay listening to the downpour as it swirled down gutters and culverts, hoping it would clear up before we set out for the dig on the following day. I fervently wanted Ita's affairs to go well. Teeming rain would not be conducive to romance and would probably prevent Brian from showing us over the site. The hypnotic drone of the rain began to lull me to sleep and I was on the verge of drifting into unconsciousness when there was a tap on the door.

I jerked awake, not sure if I had imagined it, then, as it was repeated, I got out of bed and slipped into a dressing-gown. It would be Ita, I felt sure: pleased and excited at the prospect of the following day's meeting with Brian Carbery, she was probably unable to sleep and anxious for a chat.

When I pulled the door open I was surprised to see that it was Derry who was standing there. He carried a lamp which cast shadows on his lean hollowed cheeks and I could see his white teeth glitter as he smiled sardonically. 'Do you know you look quite charming in that get-up. Déshabille quite suits you, my dear girl.'

'What do you want?' I asked sharply.

'Let's say I had insomnia and felt a little chat with you would help to pass the hours away.'

'I'm sorry,' I said, 'but it's much too late. If you have anything to say it can keep till tomorrow.'

His eyes hardened although he retained his air of smiling urbanity. 'It so happens, my dear, that I prefer to speak to you tonight—and may I remind you that you're in no position to dictate terms.'

His manner puzzled and worried me, and taking advantage of my hesitation, he pushed past me into the room. Placing the green-shaded lamp on my bedside table, he coolly sat down on the edge of the bed and regarded me appraisingly.

'Get out!' I whispered furiously. 'Suppose Rowan or Ita were to find you here at this time of night you can imagine what they would think.'

'I can well imagine, my dear, although this is not the first time I've paid you a nocturnal visit, if you remember. On that occasion, my intentions were, unflatteringly, quite honourable—but then, according to all accounts, you were Rowan's sweet unspoiled little fledgling, brought back to the ancestral home to be sheltered and cherished. It happens I know better now.'

'I can't imagine what you're talking about,' I said impatiently. 'All I know is you have no right to burst into my room at this time of night.'

'You forget I overheard your quarrel with Rowan this evening. Evidently you've been playing games with Brian Carbery in your spare time. Now what, may I ask, has he got that I haven't? If you've some time on your hands, why waste it on Ita's old flame? You'll find I'm much more interesting and can give you a better time.'

'You're talking utter rubbish,' I said angrily. 'It's true I've been speaking to Brian—but that's all. Now will you go?'

'No,' he said shortly, and leaning forward he caught my arms and pulled me towards him. 'Now listen to me! Rowan may think that Brian Carbery is taking advantage of you and that you're more sinned against than sinning, but I don't believe that for a moment, so let's get down to cases. If you come with me to Dublin we could have a good time together and, when it's over and we feel like calling it a day, part the best of friends with no hard feelings on either side. After all, why not? You've nothing to lose by leaving Raheen now: Rowan's already suspicious of you and when Emer takes over you'll be without a home anyway, for she'll make your life so wretched that you'll be glad to go, so if you've any sense you'll leap at what I may say with all due modesty is a pretty generous offer.'

His face was close to mine and with a gesture of revulsion I pulled back from him. But, clutching me tightly by the wrists, he gave my arms a vicious twist and tugged me roughly even closer. With a cry I stumbled and fell beside him on to the bed and as I struggled to free myself from his unrelenting grip I felt Derry tense. Suddenly he dropped my wrists, his attention riveted on the door.

Breathlessly I scrambled to my feet, pushing my dishevelled hair back, and glancing up saw that Rowan was watching us from the open door. He stood there in the shadows, tall and immobile in a dark maroon dressing-gown with velvet collar and cuffs and, in spite of my utter dismay, I was again reminded of his eighteenth-century ancestor.

His voice was icily contemptuous when he spoke. 'So I was wrong in thinking it was merely a flirtation you were carrying on with Brian Carbery. You're not the innocent you would like to make yourself out and no doubt Derry was all too willing to oblige. Well, you may have been clever enough to deceive that silly aunt of yours, but with me you're dealing with a very different person: get it into your head that you are not going to carry on an affair with my brother while you are under my roof. Do you understand me?'

I paled with shock at the savagery of his words, then

was filled with a burning resentment at the injustice. I tried to stammer out an explanation, but, with a final look of contempt, he turned and strode from the room.

'It looks like it was time I was taking my departure,' Derry said hurriedly. 'I never like to outstay my welcome with a lady, but if ever there's anything I can do for you, don't hesitate—and all that sort of thing——' He edged towards the door.

'Wait!' I called.

At another time his almost ludicrous expression of astonishment would have been amusing. It was quite obvious he was not used to his lady friends taking command of the situation. 'You spoke about doing something for me—well, you can. Tomorrow morning I'm leaving here. I'd like you to drive me to Daisy Tarrant's.'

'Daisy Tarrant's?' he echoed. 'But you must be completely crackers even to think of such a thing. She's a frightfully rackety old character and is the laughing-stock of the countryside. Besides,' he added, 'Rowan won't let you go—and quite right too!'

'You and Rowan appear to have agreed on one subject at least,' I said dryly. 'However, Rowan will have no say in the matter. I shall leave here early tomorrow and if you refuse to drive me I shall ask the direction in the village and go myself.'

'Oh, very well, if you insist,' she said uneasily, and as he made his departure it gave me a certain amount of satisfaction to note that he was extremely dismayed at the prospect of being involved in my revolt.

CHAPTER TEN

I WAS packing when Doreen entered with tea on the following morning. She laid down the tray and waited in surprise as I pulled open drawers and emptied the wardrobe of my few possessions. 'But what in the world are you about, miss?' she asked at last, her eyes round with astonishment.

'I'm leaving Raheen, Doreen,' I said briefly, 'and I don't want you to tell Mr Rowan anything about it. Promise me you won't.'

She nodded reluctantly, but I could see she was troubled about what she considered was disloyalty to her employer

'Don't worry, Doreen,' I added quickly, 'I'll let Mr Rowan know where I've gone later, but not now.' I simply couldn't bear another Delaney scene, I felt.

'But what about Miss Ita? Am I not to tell her either?'

With a jolt I remembered the arrangements Ita and I had made for the afternoon. 'I'll slip along to her room and explain things before I go,' I told her.

'I'm glad someone else will know,' she replied, 'otherwise no doubt I'd get all the blame for not telling him you were all set to run away.'

'Not run away, Doreen.' I smiled ruefully. 'I'm not a madcap schoolgirl, you know!'

She sniffed. 'Here you were, all right and comfortable, living with your own flesh and blood, then off you go sudden without rhyme or reason. There's no sense in it, and that's a fact.'

When I went to Ita's room she was already up and combing her hair in front of the mirror. She looked around as I entered. 'I've been thinking of changing my hairstyle, Nicola: do you think it would suit me if I wore it shoulder-length? Although Brian probably won't like it. He always said the smooth Madonna style suited me best,' she added with a happy secret smile. Then as she saw the expression on my face she said in alarm, 'What's wrong, Nicola?'

'I'm sorry, Ita, but I've decided to leave Raheen.'

Slowly she laid down her comb. 'So soon?' she said flatly. 'But why? You said last night you wouldn't be going for some time.'

'Things have changed since then,' I stated without enlarging.

'I think I understand. It's Rowan, isn't it? But what about our arrangements for this afternoon? I was counting on your coming with me.'

'There's no reason why I shouldn't. You could pick me up at Mrs Tarrant's place.'

'Oh, you're only going to Daisy's,' she said with relief. 'I was afraid you intended to go back to England.'

'There's no home for me there now,' I said flatly. Even if there were, I thought, could I bear to put the Irish Sea between myself and Rowan?

'All the same, Nicola,' she said thoughtfully, as she pinned her hair back, 'I don't imagine you'll like it at Daisy's. She's a frightfully rough diamond in her own way and, as I told you last night, her parties are really something.'

'I've heard the same thing from Derry,' I said dryly, 'but I imagine life at Raheen will have prepared me for her vagaries.'

She gave a peal of genuine amusement. 'Oh, we're in the halfpenny place compared to Daisy Tarrant. The countryside is ringing with her exploits. When it gets around that you're working for her you'll be considered birds of a feather. I suppose you haven't told Rowan of your plans?' she enquired dryly.

'No, of course not, and you mustn't tell him either,' I said quickly.

'Oh, very well. But have you made arrangements about getting there? Daisy lives a few miles outside Galway and the bus doesn't pass her place.'

'Derry has agreed to drive me,' I said quickly.

'Well, I must say that's a change for him! As a rule he doesn't believe in obliging people. However, in your case, he seems to have made an exception.' She smiled at me warmly.

To my relief she showed no signs of knowing of his invasion of my bedroom on the previous night and when I left her it was arranged she should call for me at Daisy's house in the afternoon.

I returned to my room to collect my case, then, avoiding the front of the Castle, slipped down by the back way to the courtyard.

Derry was already waiting for me and he looked a little anxious as he tossed my case into the back seat. 'We'd better get going. Rowan has just about finished breakfast and I don't want him to find me aiding and abetting you in this Daisy Tarrant venture, or he'll take an even more dim view of my activities than he already does.'

'You mean you're frightened of him?' I said contemptuously.

'You have hit the nail fair and squarely on the head,' he replied frankly as he drove through the archway from the courtyard. 'He didn't altogether blame me for last night's débâcle, for I suspect he thought you gave me a certain amount of encouragement.'

'That was fairly obvious,' I said acidly.

'However, deliberately assisting you to run off to a notorious character like Daisy is a completely different matter. You heard how he said I could return to Raheen if I got fed-up with this new job I'm taking up. Well, on more mature thought, it occurred to me that at some future date, I might be glad to return to the ancestral home. However, there's always the possibility that he may withdraw his gracious permission should he discover I'm a party to this escapade of yours.'

There was no sign of Rowan, however, as he drove past the Castle and down the avenue.

Except for a few abstracted remarks Derry was unusually silent as we drove through Galway and then took a narrow rough road through wild boggy country and turned in a narrow cart track that led to a large ramshackle home with peeling stucco: the windows were dark with grime and I could see that several slates were missing from the roof: ducks and geese waddled about the overgrown lawn and here and there through the wilderness of shrubs and weeds I caught glimpses of broken statuary and garden ornaments: a magnificent red cock ran in front of the car and Derry with an exclamation narrowly avoided running it down.

When we drew up, Daisy appeared from the side of the house, dressed in a sagging Aran-knit pullover and slacks and carrying an empty plastic basin. 'What the devil do you think you're doing, young man?' she shouted bellicosely. 'You damned nearly knocked off my prize Rhode Island Red!'

Derry laughed. 'Relax, Daisy. I've brought you a little helpmate.'

As I got out of the car Daisy regarded me a little doubtfully. 'You really mean you took me up on that offer? It sounds too good to be true. By the way,' she asked frowningly, 'I forgot to enquire if you know anything about taking care of beagles.'

'Beagles?' I repeated.

Derry laughed gleefully at my look of bewilderment. 'Daisy keeps beagles which are her joy and pride, so I hope you're well up in doggy lore.'

'I'm afraid I don't know anything about dogs,' I said.

'Never mind,' Daisy replied bracingly, 'you'll get into it in no time and I can't tell you how bucked I am that you've decided to come. I've a feeling you and I will get on like a house on fire.'

'Well, I'd better push off,' Derry said as he dumped my case on the gravel. 'Take good care of her, Daisy, or Rowan will be down on you like a ton of bricks.'

'Rowan!' she snorted bellicosely. 'He'd better stay well out of my way. If I see him around these parts I'll set the dogs on him.'

'Not Kebab, I hope!' Derry was convulsed with laughter and when he had recovered said to me sotto voce, 'Remember, if you feel you're not going to get on like the proverbial house-on-fire my offer is still open.'

'Thanks,' I said stiffly, 'but I'm quite sure I'll be able to cope.'

164

But as he drove off my heart sank as I saw the car disappear. Much as I disliked him, Derry was my last link with Raheen, for I realized that after Ita called in the afternoon my connection with the Castle would gradually peter out. Apart from the fact that Daisy made no secret of her dislike of the Delaneys I knew that Ita would be intolerant and impatient of Daisy's eccentricities.

However, even had I wanted to, it was too late now to change my mind, so I picked up my case and followed Daisy into a narrow dark hall painted in a depressing shade of pea green.

She pushed open a door. 'I want you to meet the family,' she announced cheerfully.

The room was large with grimy leaded windows and incredibly untidy. Magazines on dog lore were scattered about the dusty cretonne armchairs and sofa. On the worn scuffed carpet three loppy-eared pups fought and wrestled amidst an overturned basin of food, watched benevolently by a large extraordinary-looking dog which I guessed must be of some strange mixed breed.

'This is Kebab,' Daisy said fondly as it slowly rose from its place on the sagging sofa and flopped awkwardly towards us. 'I want you to be the best of friends. Say hello to Nicola,' she appealed coaxingly.

The enormous shaggy animal put out a paw and gazed at me with sad moist eyes. 'I call him Kebab because he's a mixture, as you can see,' she said in a confidential tone as though fearful of wounding his feelings. 'He's a little bit of this and a little bit of that.'

'He looks rather like a St Bernard,' I ventured

feebly.

'You could be right,' Daisy conceded, 'but there's a touch of the Labrador about the legs, don't you think, and I have the feeling that there's a good deal of the Pyrenean Mountain dog in his ancestry.'

Whatever Kebab's breeding, it was obvious he was completely docile and good-natured, and I began to understand Derry's amusement at the idea that it was this dog Daisy had threatened to set on Rowan.

'Dear old boy,' Daisy rumpled his shaggy ears. 'What should I do without him? These are rather delicate,' she went on as the pups scampered towards her, 'but the rest of the litter is doing well. I'm raising them for the local harriers. By the way, you must join, Nicola,' she said earnestly. 'When I was your age I thought nothing of following the hounds over hedges and ditches. It's good for the figure too. Although I must say,' she added, looking at me critically, 'that you've nothing to complain of along those lines.' She led the way outdoors and showed me around a maze of decrepit sheds and pens that housed the dogs and the rest of the litter and explained to me that my duties would be to feed and—on the days when they were not hunting—exercise the dogs.

I listened appalled as she explained the peculiarities of each individual animal. I found it impossible to distinguish one from the other and realized I wouldn't be able to remember her instructions. As she spoke with loving pleasure on her charges I guessed how quick she would be to show her displeasure if I failed in my duties—as I most surely would.

Afterwards we had tea, surrounded by the pups and with Kebab going from one to the other of us pushing his huge head on to our laps and rolling his mournful eyes upwards until he received a titbit.

Daisy poured tea from a china teapot. 'It's supposed to be an antique,' she exclaimed abruptly. 'I'd have put it in the auction if my late husband hadn't been so crazy about it. It seems it had been in his family for generations—although personally I can't understand why people hoard up possessions: it doesn't make any sense to me: they only gather dust and are damned depressing.'

She handed a biscuit to Kebab who crunched it noisily on the carpet. 'They say Raheen Castle is full of gloomy old-fashioned furniture and is haunted into the bargain: it's time Rowan took a bride who would pitch out all that rubbish and brighten the place up.'

Somehow the idea of Raheen, with its old mellow furniture and air of antiquity, brightened up didn't appeal to me and Daisy said with more perspicuity than I should have given her credit for, 'Although I expect, if you had any say in it, you'd keep it as it is, wouldn't you?'

'Yes,' I admitted.

'I do hope you're not a silly romantic sort of girl, because if so you certainly won't shake down here. There's nothing annoys me more than a girl who's dreamy and gets the vapours and hasn't the remotest idea what side her bread is buttered on. Well, it's just as well that Emer has set her cap at Rowan, for she'll be a breath of fresh air at that old mausoleum. She won't be mistress of Raheen very long before she tosses out all that junk and makes the place really comfortable.'

This confirmed so exactly my own views of Emer's

plans that I felt myself growing more and more depressed.

'Yes,' Daisy continued, in her stentorian ringing tones, 'I'd say Rowan will plump for Emer and her father will certainly give her a handsome dowry. Emer has made no secret of the fact that she's straining at the leash. Well, I'm not surprised, for although I can't stand the man I'd say Rowan has a dangerous charm. You didn't fall for him?' she asked bluntly.

I hastily bent my head and became engrossed in placing a piece of cake in Kebab's cavernous mouth.

'Don't bother to answer.' She brushed crumbs from her mouth. 'I think I get the picture. You quarrelled with him and came here in a fit of the sulks.' She sighed and stood up. 'I might have known it was too good to be true. This means, I suppose, that you'll go back to Raheen when there's a reconciliation and I'll lose a kennel-maid.'

'Oh no,' I said quickly, 'I'll never return to Raheen. As you say, Rowan will marry Emer and there will be no place for me there.'

In spite of myself I felt my voice tremble and with a movement of rough compassion she clapped me on the shoulder. 'Now you're talking sense. When you've been here a few months you'll forget all about Rowan and Raheen. I'll try to make things as pleasant as possible and not fly off the handle too much and you'll find we'll shake down quite comfortably. Now if you're finished, I'll show you through the house, then take you to your quarters.'

Talking volubly and accompanied by Kebab who padded heavily behind us, she showed me from one desolate ramshackle room to another. Here and there on the upper floor were strategically placed basins and these, Daisy explained, were intended to catch the drips from the roof when it rained. 'I had some men working on it,' she admitted, 'but we didn't see eye to eye. Much too damned touchy; wouldn't take a few home truths; downed tools and left in the huff.'

I could well imagine what Daisy would consider a few home truths and I realized how unlikely it was I would be with her on a permanent basis.

When we reached my bedroom I was pleasantly surprised to see it was a comfortable little room under the eaves. 'The roof doesn't leak here, so you'll be high and dry,' she announced with satisfaction.

An old-fashioned ewer and basin ornamented with a design of violets stood on a stand in a corner. 'Perhaps you'd like to wash and brush up,' she said graciously, 'and then when you come down I'll show you how to make up the dogs' feed.' She stood there looking raw-boned and awkward, then added, 'I know it's not up to Raheen standards, but I'm rather a slapdash sort of person.'

There was something touching about her helplessness and I said on impulse, 'Would you like me to tidy up things generally, Daisy?'

'What do you mean,' she asked doubtfully.

'Oh, the sitting-room, for instance. I could tidy up and polish the furniture and make it generally——' I had been about to say 'habitable', but stopped in time.

Daisy brightened. 'That's a damn good idea.' Then she stopped and frowned. 'As long as you don't make Kebab and the pups unhappy. They're used to the run of the house and I'd hate them to be miserable.'

When I had promised to give Kebab and the pups

every consideration, she departed and I changed into an old skirt and jumper for my chores.

Later on, when I had tidied up the living-room, polished the brass ornaments, and was busily dusting the furniture and revelling in the way the room was gradually assuming a welcoming glow, I heard a car draw up outside and saw Emer emerge. She was alone and after a quick and disdainful glance at the surrounding dilapidation she picked her way towards the hall door and knocked.

There was no sign of Daisy and for a moment I hesitated, wondering whether to go in search of her, then pulling from my head the scarf I had tied about my hair before beginning work, I went towards the door conscious of feeling hot and grimy and aware that my hands were stained with metal polish.

Emer looked elegant and self-possessed in a fur-trimmed coat, her hair loose beneath a tiny pillbox hat of blond mink. For a moment she regarded me from head to toe, then said in a tone of surprise, 'What on earth have you been doing to yourself?'

'I've been cleaning up,' I said crisply. 'Do you want to see Daisy?'

'See Daisy?' she scoffed. 'My dear girl, we cordially dislike each other. I was hoping she'd be engaged with those ghastly animals of hers, as there's something I want to say to you.' I hesitated and she said sweetly, 'As we appear to be alone don't you think it would be a good idea to ask me in?'

Reluctantly I led the way into the living-room and Emer looked about in faint surprise. 'Well, I must say you've made some improvements. The last time I called on Daisy was when Father was doing some business with her and the place was really disgustingly neglected.' She shuddered with revulsion. 'And there was a dreadful shaggy dog with an enormous head that positively gave me the horrors.'

I nodded. 'Kebab.'

'Kebab,' she echoed. 'I remember now; that's what she calls the brute. Frankly he looked to me like a rather neglected hearthrug.'

'I know he's not particularly pretty,' I admitted, 'but he's an affectionate, lovable old thing.'

'You appear to be becoming quite a fan of his,' she said acidly. 'Personally I think Daisy carries her love of animals much too far. However, I haven't come here to discuss her peculiarities.'

'In that case what exactly did you come for?' I asked. Daisy might reappear at any minute and I dreaded the scene that might ensue when the two antagonists met.

She flung herself back on one of the armchairs, and crossing her legs regarded me narrowly. 'I heard you'd walked out on Rowan, and I must say I'm curious to know the reason why. I couldn't get anything out of Ita.' She frowned and opening her bag took out cigarettes and lighter. 'For some reason or other the girl has changed towards me: she's not half so eager to please. Anyway, she didn't give any sensible explanation.'

I shook my head at the proffered gold cigarette case. 'Perhaps that's because I didn't give her one,' I said quietly.

She smoked thoughtfully. 'But you must have had some reason for leaving so suddenly. People in your position simply don't drop everything and walk out and go to Daisy Tarrant—of all people—unless they have a pretty good reason.'

'My reason is absolutely none of your business,' I said curtly, 'and now, Emer, if you don't mind, I'll get on with my work.'

'I can't imagine why you're reticent about your motives for leaving Raheen,' she persisted. 'After all, it was fairly obvious you were head over heels in love with Rowan.'

I turned away and slowly drew a duster over an already gleaming table so that she could not see how her words had jolted me.

'And you needn't bother to deny it,' she added sharply. 'It was written all over you in large letters. Oh, you may have thought you were very clever in hiding it, but I saw through you right from the beginning. That's why I can't understand your leaving like this. I should imagine there's nothing you'd like better than living under the same roof as your beloved!' Her tone was contemptuous.

I laid down the duster and regarded her with sudden new knowledge. 'You don't really love Rowan, do you?' I said slowly.

She blew a cloud of smoke thinly and laughed a little uneasily. 'Need you be so intense? No, I suppose I don't really love him—in a dewy-eyed sort of way, but Rowan is the only man I've ever wanted to marry. What I feel for him is stronger and more lasting than the romantic notions of a girl brought up in suburbia —without any real experience of the world,' she added.

At this moment I saw Kebab lumbering through the open door: he padded towards Emer's reclining figure and sniffed at the hand which was dangling over the edge of the chair with his wet nose.

With a scream Emer leapt to her feet and backed fearfully.

Kebab, a puzzled look on his enormous foolish face at this unfriendly reception, followed her.

Emer edged behind the sofa. 'Call the ugly brute off, will you, Nicola!' she shrilled.

It was at this moment that Daisy chose to enter, her face growing a dusky pink with anger as she overheard this unflattering description of her darling. 'What do you mean, "ugly brute", Emer Lacey? Why, Kebab wouldn't hurt a fly, would you, pet?' She put her arm about Kebab's neck and kissed him affectionately on the top of his head. 'Poor old chap, he's quite hurt. I can see it in his dear gentle eyes. And do stop yelling, girl, will you?' she added loudly. 'You're making an utter fool of yourself.'

As Kebab flopped down on the carpet and blinked his eyes sleepily, Emer regained her composure and for a few moments it looked as if she fully intended to resume her interrogation. Daisy however interrupted aggressively, 'And just why have you honoured us with a visit?'

Emer shrugged. 'Oh, I happened to be passing and thought I'd drop in and see how Nicola's doing.'

'Utter piffle!' Daisy informed her shortly. 'You've come because you want to know why Nicola left Raheen so suddenly. Isn't that it? Well, that's a question I didn't ask her myself and I've a better right to know than you have, so why don't you mind your own business for a change?'

'Really!' Emer gave a trill of resentful laughter. 'You've always been plain-spoken, but there's no necessity to be so abominably rude!'

'I'll be as rude as I like if you attempt to pester Nicola about something that's no concern of yours. And now don't you think it would be a good idea if you took yourself off?' Daisy concluded bluntly.

Emer jumped to her feet, her eyes sparkling with anger and was on the point of flouncing out of the room, when a car drove up and Ita got out.

'And just what is Ita Delaney doing here?' Daisy asked thoughtfully. 'I suppose Rowan sent her here to try and get you to go back to Raheen.'

I was on the point of denying this and explaining the real reason for Ita's visit, when I realized that Emer was listening with avid interest. Once she had heard of our plans for the afternoon she would not hesitate to inform Rowan.

However, it was Ita herself who gave away our plans. She stood on the doorstep a little diffidently and explained to Daisy why she had called, and as Emer and I joined them we were in time to hear Daisy say gruffly, 'About time too you put Brian Carbery out of his misery. You've kept that unfortunate man on a string much too long, and if you've any gumption you'll keep Rowan out of it.'

'You mean you're going to see Brian Carbery?' Emer asked sharply.

'Yes,' Ita replied simply. 'Last night I was thinking things over and I realized I've been a fool. If Brian still wants me I'll marry him, and it won't be a hole-and-corner affair. We'll get married here in Raheen, and neither Rowan nor anyone else will be able to prevent it.'

'GOOD for you!' Daisy crowed, 'and I'll be glad to see Rowan taken off his high horse. Well, I'll leave you young people to have a chat. I've to make up the turkey mash and can't hang around all day chin-wagging.' She wandered away around the side of the house, having apparently forgotten that she had already ordered Emer from her property.

As soon as she had gone, Ita turned to her friend and said impulsively, 'Won't you come with us, Emer?'

Emer laughed shortly. 'I'm afraid it's simply not in character for me to play gooseberry for another couple. You see, I admit it—I'm so used to being the centre of the picture that I don't enjoy playing second fiddle— even for you,' she added with an air of ingenuousness.

Ita looked disappointed as she watched Emer pull on her driving gloves and slide behind the wheel, and I had a feeling of foreboding as her low red car swung down the rutted cart-track and disappeared from view. I knew she was hurrying back to convey her discoveries to Rowan.

Quickly I changed, pulled on a coat and went to ask Daisy if she would have any objection to my accompanying Ita. I found her in an outhouse stirring a huge cauldron of bran mash with a wooden stick: smoke curled from the cigar that was firmly clenched between her teeth and about her feet wandered geese and ducks pecking eagerly at the drops of mash that fell to the earthen floor.

She instantly gave her assent. 'Although mind you,' she added earnestly, 'I wanted to show you how to prepare the turkey mash. They're tricky birds to rear and if they're not roosting in the trees they're dropping dead from some disease or other: you just can't be too careful when it comes to turkeys.'

I promised her I'd watch closely next time she prepared the turkey mash and hurried back to Ita, who was already behind the wheel and eager to go. As we drove off she glanced about at Daisy's dilapidated property and I could see she was offended by the general air of seedy neglect.

'Don't you hate it here, Nicola?' she asked hesitantly after a few moments. 'I know I should. Apart from that, Daisy would get on my nerves, she's so boisterous and hearty. We'd probably spend our time exchanging insults.'

I smiled. 'You forget I'm not really a Delaney, so I'm not so quick to lose my temper. Besides, I rather like her: I don't really believe she's as tough as she pretends: I think she's lonely and misses her husband much more than she thought possible.'

Ita smiled. 'Barney Tarrant was hopelessly henpecked. I expect he took to collecting antiques as a sort of defence so as to have one interest she couldn't take over.' She paused, then added thoughtfully, 'I should hate to turn out like Daisy and ruin everything for Brian and myself.'

'Turn out like Daisy?' I echoed. There was so little resemblance between the raucous, rawboned woman and this calm madonna-faced girl that I laughed.

'You needn't laugh,' she said gravely. 'You must have noticed how frightfully self-willed and obstinate the Delaneys are—especially Rowan. Although it's all right for him: Emer will be well able to look out for herself when they marry. But Brian is different: he's so gentle and civilized and utterly in control of himself!'

When they marry! I felt my heart sink at the words. So Ita had no doubt that Emer and her brother would be man and wife! It was stupidly unrealistic of me to care so much, I told myself as I felt my throat tighten and remembered that this might be the last opportunity I would have of carrying out Rowan's request concerning his sister.

I began nervously, dreading that she would resent what she might consider my interference, but to my relief she listened without rancour as I told her how Rowan had visited a Dublin surgeon on her behalf.

'Rowan actually did that?' she asked wonderingly. 'I can hardly believe he cares enough. I think that's what made me so resentful: he seemed to be so utterly indifferent to the wrong he did me.'

'He cares very much,' I said gently. 'Much more than you have realized. And you will see this surgeon, won't you?'

She hesitated. 'Yes, I suppose so.' Her tone was grudging, but I was not deceived and I knew she fully intended to meet her brother halfway.

A mist of cold rain swept the countryside as we approached the excavations. From the distance it was quite easy to see the great cairn that rose from the crest of a ridge on the hillside. 'It seems it's a passage grave built about 2000 B.C,' Ita explained, 'and of course Brian's crazy about it and can brood happily over a granite slab. I was beginning to learn something about

177

his work, because he used to show me everything he discovered and explain it to me. Now I'll be able to catch up with this season's finds—if all goes well between us, of course!' But her happy face told me she had no real doubts.

We drove up to a small wooden hut that had obviously been used for storing tools and Brian hurried forward eagerly. As Ita got out of the car looking serenely beautiful their eyes met in a long look that made speech unnecessary.

Immediately he led us into the hut which he had so obviously painstakingly furbished for our reception. A small stove made it pleasantly warm and a coffee pot bubbled above the red coals. A large bunch of pink chrysanthemums was arranged haphazardly in the centre of a rough table, and cups and saucers and plates of sandwiches and cakes on lace doilies completed his arrangement.

He watched eagerly for our reactions to these preparations. 'I know it's not much, but it's the best I could do in the circumstances.'

'It's beautiful,' Ita said happily.

'I came across some basin stones I'd like to show you, Ita,' he began eagerly.

'Basin stones,' she repeated vaguely as she crossed to the table and rearranged the chrysanthemums with an air of almost maternal indulgence.

'Don't you remember what they are?'

It was so clear that he feared she was indifferent that she said quickly, 'I'm sorry, Brian, but then I've grown so rusty in the past year——'

'In that case you'd make someone like me an extremely unsatisfactory wife,' he said softly. Again their eyes met in a long look that made me aware that I was the outsider. They had forgotten my very presence and were in a magical world of their own making.

A smile dimpled Ita's cheeks. 'Perhaps I could make up for my deficiencies by being very much in love,' she whispered.

I glanced away, more unhappy than I had been since I left Raheen. Outside the rain had grown heavier and poured down in a drenching downpour. Soon I would be returning to Daisy and her haphazard existence and inevitably we would come to the parting of the ways, for Daisy was unlikely to get on with anyone without ultimately quarrelling.

'I thought perhaps we could have something to eat after I've taken you into the cairn,' he said, turning to me. 'Although it's a pity it has rained so much lately as conditions won't be ideal.' He took candles from a cupboard and reaching down one of the heavy waterproof coats that were piled on a peg by the door he threw it around my shoulders. As he was about to take down a waterproof for Ita she said with an air of ingenuousness, 'Why don't you show Nicola the basin stones? I know she'd be awfully interested, wouldn't you?' she appealed with a conspiratorial glance in my direction, 'and I'll have hot coffee ready for you when you return.'

'A typical display of feminine cunning,' Brian told her. 'You're simply anxious to avoid getting your shoes wet.' But it was clear he understood her motive and there was hardly any need for her to say softly, 'I have all the time in the world to see them now, Brian darling.' A time when he and she would be alone together, I thought with something like envy.

'All right then, and I'll be grateful, Nicola, if you even simulate interest in my hobby-horse,' he told me as we turned towards the door.

As we climbed the ridge towards the great cairn, there was something sinister-looking about the great pile that reared above us. We crept into a small square entrance leading into a narrow dank passage, and here we lit our candles. As we moved further into the centre of the vast mound, the flickering flames illuminated the stone slabs that lined the sides of the passage and occasionally Brian would stop and enthusiastically hold his candle high to point out stones crudely carved with serpents or strange zigzag patterns. There was something awesome and rather terrifying in the knowledge that these scrawls had been made about four thousand years previously and I found it difficult to share his enthusiasm.

'The funeral chamber is at the end of the passage,' he explained as we slowly progressed deeper and deeper and the roof with its shelving corbelled slabs grew progressively higher. Except for the water which dripped steadily from the roof there was an uncanny silence.

'Here we are,' he announced at last, hurrying forward and shining his candle into a sloping chamber which reached about twenty feet high at its centre point. 'It's considered the finest corbelled vault in Western Europe!' He sounded so proud that I was ashamed of how horrified I felt as I gazed around. Water trickled from the roof and formed deep puddles on the floor and the air was dank and smelled of mould and decay. Then it struck me to ask him about the basin stones he had mentioned to Ita. These, it turned out, were situated in the low recesses formed by the roof and were of sandstone and granite. Their contents, he explained, which had probably been bone beads, pottery and stone pendants, had been looted by the Norsemen many centuries previously.

But it was not the sort of place one would linger in and I gave a sigh of relief as we turned and headed back for the outside world again. It was evident that in the meanwhile a storm had begun to rage, for water now poured in torrents in the cracks in the corbelled roof and there was the muffled roar of thunder.

Brian frowned as we hurried forward. 'It's time we got out of here. We've had roof falls occasionally, although fortunately there was no one inside at the time.'

I followed closely in his footsteps, the uneasiness I had felt since we had first entered the mound springing into alarm at his words. At length the flickering candles illuminated a lozenge design on one of the stone slabs Brian had pointed out to me soon after we had stepped through the narrow opening: so we must be near the entrance, I thought with relief, as I recognized the pattern. It was just then we heard a dull roar and the sound of crashing stone reverberating along the passage. We looked at each other in alarm.

'What—what was that?' I asked tremulously, trying to control the quaver in my voice.

'It sounds as if the roof has caved in near the entrance,' he replied grimly. 'However, we'd better stop speculating and find out!' But as he spoke I saw the lines of his face grow deeply etched with anxiety.

We were not long in discovering that he had been right in his surmise. We hurried forward to find that a great slab of roughly hewn stone, with rubble and debris, completely blocked the passage ahead. Brian studied it for a few moments, then carefully propped his candle on a piece of stone. 'If only we could lower it a little,' I heard him mutter. He grasped an edge of the great slab and pulled, but his thin scholarly frame didn't look equal to the task: again he pulled with all his strength, then suddenly I heard him gasp.

'What's wrong?' I asked anxiously.

He rubbed his shoulder ruefully. 'I seem to have hurt myself. It looks as if I've outstayed my welcome here and the spirits are bent on gaining vengeance. I'm afraid there's nothing we can do, Nicola, but wait to be rescued. As soon as Ita realizes that there's something wrong, she'll send for help.'

'But where to?' I asked doubtfully. I had seen nothing but an occasional whitewashed cottage as we had driven towards the cairn.

'The mine, of course,' he answered. 'Rowan will send out men: they're used to working in these conditions and will know exactly how to handle the cave-in.'

The prospect of being rescued by Rowan alarmed me even more than the long wait that lay ahead in this damp musty passage. We spread out our waterproofs and sat down, each of us silent and busy with our own thoughts. Hours seemed to pass and then with a little stab of terror I noticed that our candles were slowly but surely flickering down to shapeless stumps. Shortly afterwards they went out, and in the utter darkness the dank walls seemed to press on me and I had the horrifying conviction that we had been ignored and forgotten by the outside world. Brian's joking words about the spirits which must inhabit this place seemed to echo in my mind. Angered by our intrusion, were they jubilantly exulting in our fate? Perhaps we would soon join them and the mound would become our burial chamber too.

As I put my hand up to prevent a scream of horror and revulsion I heard a sound of faint activity beyond the rock fall.

Brian seemed to hear it at the same moment and sprang to his feet in excitement. 'It's the men from the mines, and they're using picks. I'm amazed they've managed to come so soon.'

'I think I know how it happened,' I said slowly. 'Ita told Emer we were coming here. You see, she trusted her, but of course she immediately told Rowan.'

'It's not often treachery has such pleasant results,' he said dryly. 'However, for once I'll be pleased to see that arrogant brother of Ita's.'

Now, however, that I was no longer terrified of a horrifying fate I began to feel apprehensive of Rowan's arrival. He would already be furious, I realized, that I had encouraged his sister to meet Brian Carbery. What would be his reaction when he discovered that not only had I deliberately ignored his wishes but had also managed to put myself in a position where he had to organize rescue operations for Brian Carbery and myself?

As the sounds grew stronger and began to reverberate in great hollow booms along the passage I stood up, trembling with nervous tension. Suddenly the passage-way was filled with light as the stone was thrust aside and we found ourselves in the blaze of the torches Rowan's workmen had rigged up to illuminate their rescue work. For a moment I could hear Rowan's voice directing operations and Ita's scream, 'Brian, you're hurt!' before the lights seemed to expand and contract, then swirl in ever widening circles, and it was as though I were falling into a vast and dark abyss.

When I opened my eyes it was to find myself once more in the hut. I gazed round, dazed and shocked. There was no sign of Ita or Brian and I wondered vaguely where they might be, but was unable to focus my thoughts clearly.

Rowan crossed to the stove and filled a mug with hot coffee. 'Here, take this,' he said abruptly, pushing it into my hand.

I sipped at the hot liquid and gradually felt my confidence return. 'Where is Ita?' I demanded anxiously.

'Quite your old self, aren't you?' he remarked dryly. 'Back at the old stand, organizing Ita's life for her and bringing the star-crossed lovers together. For your information Brian has been taken to the local hospital with a minor injury to his shoulder. Needless to say, Ita, all solicitude, insisted on accompanying him. It appears,' he added dryly, 'that she's deeply in love and I'd say fully intends to marry him.'

'It's what she wanted,' I retorted with as much firmness as I could muster.

He regarded me sombrely for a long moment, then said, 'Yes, you're quite right. It's what she wanted. I did wrong to interfere in the first place. Brian Carbery probably loves her as much as he loves any woman: archaeology comes first with him, I'd say, and a woman would come a poor second to any really interesting discovery.'

It was true, of course, I admitted to myself, reluctant

to concede him right. Brian Carbery's first love was archaeology. I was confident, however, that Ita would play a discreet second fiddle and would revel in her role. Well, at least when she had driven off with him she had had the heartwarming knowledge that she was close to the man she loved; that her future had been settled!

I looked around the small desolate hut: Brian's carefully arranged table was now a jumble of assorted mugs and half-eaten sandwiches and the flowers Ita had arranged with such happy self-confidence had been pushed into a convenient corner. Evidently Rowan's men had made this their headquarters during the rescue operations.

I was suddenly made aware of how much time and expense our little adventure had cost him. 'I'm sorry we were such trouble to you,' I began haltingly, 'especially as we were not in danger.'

He shrugged and opening the lid of the stove tossed in a piece of wood. 'Nevertheless I couldn't leave you languishing in the interior of a megalithic grave. For all I knew you might have had a fit of screaming hysterics.'

'I hadn't,' I said pallidly, feeling flattened and depressed by his detached and matter-of-fact attitude, yet what had I expected? I asked myself. Had some part of me harboured the ridiculous hope that his attitude towards me would have undergone a dramatic change just because I had been incarcerated for a short time in the tumulus?

He regarded me thoughtfully. 'I shouldn't have said that. You're not really the type to have screaming hysterics, are you?'

I had the horrible feeling that perhaps he could sense my bitter disappointment at his attitude and recklessly said, 'I suppose you mean I'm not the feminine type? No doubt if I'd been Emer you would have felt very differently?'

He raised his eyebrows and said sardonically, 'It's unlikely Emer would have been foolish enough to get herself into such a pickle. Somehow I don't see her wandering around a burial chamber with a candle. Her interests, I imagine, would lie along very different lines.'

I gazed at him doubtfully. There was an ambiguity about his words that made me uncertain of his real attitude. However, there was no mistaking his next remark, 'Well, if you're fully recovered I suppose I'd better take you back.'

'Back!' For an instant I had the wild hope he might mean Raheen, then felt a sick dismay clutch at me when he said, 'To Daisy, of course! Where else? She has been ringing Raheen, worrying about you, and we'd better let her know as soon as possible that you're safe and sound.'

'Yes, of course,' I said mechanically. When Daisy had been told of the accident that had befallen me, her first reaction had probably been alarm lest she lost her new kennel-maid, I told myself dispiritedly.

He helped me on with my coat and in silence we left the hut. The rain had stopped and a full moon was glowing, a pale silver sphere in the clear washed sky, and as we drove through the sleeping countryside I gazed longingly at the cosy whitewashed cottages, set in stone-walled fields, dreaming beneath the moonlight. How content I would be, sheltered beneath a cosy thatched roof as long as I was with the man I loved! I glanced briefly at Rowan, but his eyes were fixed on the dark road ahead and I looked away as I felt tears fill my eyes. Somehow the thought that I was to return to Daisy Tarrant and her rough untidy existence seemed unbearable. I shivered and pressed myself disconsolately against the door.

'Well,' he remarked, without taking his eyes off the road, 'you're remarkably untalkative for a woman! Aren't you going to give me a résumé of your life with Daisy?'

'No, why should I?' I replied with a returning flicker of antagonism. 'Daisy may be eccentric, but at least she means well, and has shown me kindness in her own way.'

I saw him smile. 'So you are also loyal, Nicola!'

'I don't know what you mean,' I said a little sulkily.

'Just that Daisy can consider herself fortunate that she had the luck to grab your services when she had the chance. It looks as if I played straight into her hands last night when you and I aired our grievances. But I mustn't begrudge her her good fortune,' he added as we turned into the rough track that led to the house. 'My loss is her gain, as it were.'

Speechless with misery, I stared ahead.

'I can see a couple of turkeys roosting in that sycamore tree,' Rowan continued conversationally. 'Is it one of our duties to rescue the stupid creatures?'

'I expect it will be,' I replied hollowly, 'when I've been here long enough and have learned how to handle them.'

'I can see it will probably be years before you master the intricacies of turkey psychology. However, you'd be amazed at how the time flies when one is energetically occupied.' He drew up outside the house.

Immediately Daisy appeared in a sagging dressing-gown with Kebab at her heels. She looked cross and anxious and her hair was an untidy bush about her strong-featured face. 'And just what have you been doing with yourself, Nicola?' she demanded loudly. 'Do you realize I've been worrying myself sick about you?'

'Well, here she is, safe and sound,' Rowan said.

Immediately she rounded on him indignantly. 'And what are you doing here, Rowan Delaney?'

'Bringing back your kennel-maid,' he said calmly. 'Isn't that what you wanted?'

Daisy felt in her pocket and lit a cigar thoughtfully. 'With a bit of experience she would make the best kennel-maid I've ever had, but at the same time I don't want to stand in her way. She's in love with you, and if you've the smallest scrap of gumption, Rowan Delaney, you'll marry the girl. She's worth a thousand Emer Laceys.'

I could feel my cheeks glow with embarrassment. How typical of Daisy to put me in such an unbearable situation!

I opened the car door and was on the point of scurrying to the shelter of the house when Rowan put a restraining hand on my arm. 'Do you know, Daisy,' he remarked conversationally, 'I think that might be a very good idea. For once you and I see eye to eye, so you'll have no objection if I take her back to Raheen.'

There was a long pause as Daisy digested this and I glanced at him desperately, wondering if it were simply a joke at her expense.

'You mean you're definitely not going to get hitched up to Emer Lacey?' she asked at last.

'As it happens, for some time now I've had no intention of doing any such thing.'

Daisy's face softened as she turned to me. 'I'll come to your wedding, my dear,' she said gruffly, 'if you'd like me to.'

I gazed at her, dazed with wonder and happiness, and Kebab, raising himself on his hind legs, placed his enormous head through the window and blinked benevolently at me, then followed his mistress back to the house.

Daisy stood in the open doorway and waved as Rowan turned the car, and we drove off leaving Daisy and her strange menage far behind us.

'You're crying,' he said wonderingly, as he pulled me close to his side.

'With happiness,' I gulped, and added inanely, 'Now I won't have to rescue those wretched turkeys.'

He smiled. 'Did you really tell Daisy you were in love with me?'

'Of course not,' I said primly. 'At least, not exactly.'

'I see, so you're being cautious. Well, would you be more forthcoming if I told you that I love you?'

'But when?' I asked eagerly.

'When?' He raised his eyebrows quizzically. 'Now what do you mean by that?'

'When did you first begin to love me?' I asked a little shyly.

'From the first moment I saw you, although your hair was tied back with a rubber band.'

I laughed. 'So you noticed even that!'

'But of course the smallest detail is important when

you meet a girl who looks like being the only one in your life. I also noticed that you glared at me very fiercely. However, I didn't let it discourage me too much, as I suspected you were very lonely and very frightened.'

'But not any more,' I whispered happily, 'because I'm going home.'

Ahead lay the road to Raheen, and already its towers gleamed silver in the moonlight.